BAYOU SUNSET

AN AGENTS OF HIS NOVEL

SHEILA KELL

Cunningham Publishing, USA

Titles by Sheila Kell

Author's Note

This narrative unfolds predominantly in a quaint, secluded backwoods town populated by colorful local characters. This setting serves as the canvas on which I have woven the unique linguistic charm of Cajun-French and Cajun-English into the dialogue. While I don't claim to be an authority on these dialects, I have thoughtfully integrated and adapted them to enrich the storytelling experience. For your reference, I've compiled a list of these terms should their meanings be unclear within the narrative context—some are loosely translated.

Au revoir—Bye, Goodbye, See you later
Bateau—boat
Beaucoup—a lot, a bunch
Bien—good
Bien amusant—good/fun time
Bière—beer
Bon—good
Bonjour—Hello
Bonsoir—Good evening
Ça va—okay, fine, good
Chèr—friend (male)
Chère—friend (female)
Couyon—Crazy or stupid person
Da—the
Demain soir—tomorrow night
Deux—Two
Dix—Ten
Encore—again
Et—and
Frère—brother
Huit—eight

If you please—Please

Mais—but

Mais non—but no

Mais oui—but yes

Maman—Mom

Mamau—Mom (slang-endearment)

Merci—Thank you, Thanks

Merde—a vulgar expression or exclamation of frustration

Mère—Mother

Moi—me

Mon ami—my friend

Mon amour—my love

Mon Dieu! —My God!

Mon frères—my brothers

Mon Gason—my son

Non—no

Oui—Yes, Okay

Paroles du village—Talk of the town (loosely)

Père—Father

Petite fille—young girl/lady

Que—What

Resser—Calm down

Sisit—sis (informal)

Soir—night

Souer—sister

Trois—Three

Un—One

Une bouille d'écrevisses—The crawfish festival

Une heure—an hour

Ya—You (and variants)

Chapter One

"MAYBE WE SHOULD waterboard him."

Steve "Romeo" Smith considered his teammate Brad Hamilton's advice. As Chief Interrogator at Hamilton Investigation and Security, or HIS for short, Romeo knew the family's rules on interrogations, as did Brad, who had created said rules.

Waterboarding was forbidden. However, in this instance, the tango—a suspected terrorist—didn't know they wouldn't torture him physically. A little mind fuck, though, was not out of the question.

Romeo had mastered skills beyond a traditional field agent as a former, deeply entrenched FBI interrogator. While waterboarding hadn't been one of them, he had put into practice many questionable techniques to retrieve the information necessary to save lives. Techniques even the Hamilton brothers wouldn't allow him to conduct due to the severity of the actions utilized. So, he had to retrieve info the old-fashioned way—with questioning, deceit, and intimidation.

While not his and Brad's first rodeo together, he would play along with the Hamilton brother. Romeo narrowed his eyes at the suspect, then slowly nodded in agreement to Brad's suggestion.

Brad laughed maniacally and slipped from the room, leaving Romeo alone with the tango.

Bernie Jackson, the tango, had attempted to bomb one of the radio stations owned by Kate Hamilton, Romeo's big boss's wife. Sure, they should have turned him over to the police after they caught him in the act. And they eventually would. Right now, though, they needed to know who sent Bernie. In their brief investigation, it became apparent that Bernie wasn't talented enough to create a bomb. Plus, there were no bomb-making items at Bernie's residence but a deposit of $10,000 into his checking account.

Romeo noted Bernie's sweat—a sure sign of his nervousness. "What be wrong, Bernie? Are ya afraid of a little water?" He smiled. What he had been told gave the recipient a grim outlook.

"You can't do this. I've done nothing wrong. Please, you have to let me go," Bernie insisted as he struggled in the chair he had been zip-tied to. All he managed to do was move the chair around, which didn't bother Romeo because he knew it had to hurt where the ties touched skin every time Bernie struggled.

Standing, Romeo stretched like nothing phased him. After a fake yawn, he said, "Sure, we can. Remember, no police, no rules. We can do as we wish." It was a lie, but he'd learned to lie easily after years of this work. Sometimes, he hated that he had mastered that skill, but he kept the deceit in the interrogation room.

"Help! Help me! They're trying to kill me."

Romeo closed his eyes and slowly shook his head as if to tsk the man. "I've already told ya this room is sound-proofed. All ya doing is giving me a headache. Ya don't want to see me angry, do ya, Bernie?"

With a whimper, Bernie shook his head. "I can't tell you. He said he'd kill me. Please, you have to let me go."

Well, well. At least Bernie told them he had been hired. It was funny what fake threats would do to a man, especially one delivering trouble. Romeo hovered over the shaking man. "Who will kill ya? Besides me, if ya don't tell me who hired ya?"

"I— You— I—" Bernie stumbled out and fell silent. He stopped struggling and dropped his head in defeat.

Romeo narrowed his eyes at the man. "Tell us who hired ya, and we'll protect ya against him." So far, all they knew was that it was a male.

Bernie looked up, wouldn't look Romeo in the eye, and shook his head. "No, I can't," he cried.

With a stone-cold heart that he wore during interrogations, Romeo stood there watching the tears slide down Bernie's face. He didn't care that the man was scared. The man was guilty as shit and could have killed others. It had been pure luck that the security guard caught him placing the bomb before Bernie could arm it.

Hearing heavy footsteps coming toward the room, Romeo thinned his lips. "Last chance. Brad be on his way back to take ya to be waterboarded." To make things worse, he leaned down to Bernie's ear and whispered, "It be a specialty of ours."

As expected, Bernie peed his pants. Romeo stood and stepped back as the puddle pooled at the man's feet. He hated to scare someone to that extreme, but it was sometimes necessary.

Romeo headed toward the door to open it for Brad. As he took the steps, he mentally counted: one, two, three, four.

"Okay, okay," Bernie said with a defeated tone. "Okay."

Romeo smiled, then forced a nonchalant look before turning back to Bernie. "*Oui*?"

"First, you have to promise you'll protect me," Bernie demanded.

With a quizzical raise of an eyebrow, Romeo nodded shortly. "If ya tell us the truth." He angled his head toward the door. "Ya have until Brad returns to spill ya guts."

Eyes wide, Bernie cried, "Wait!"

They had this man, and it hadn't been that difficult. Once they had the information, they would protect him, but HIS would also turn him over to the police after they caught the mastermind.

Brad walked into the room with a grim look on his face.

Romeo cocked his head in question.

"You need to come with me," Brad said to Romeo.

Staring at Brad, Romeo couldn't believe Brad had deviated from their well-developed tactic. He was supposed to enter and state the tub was ready.

"Now," Brad demanded.

Disbelief and curiosity wormed their way into Romeo. What in the world was going on? Brad had to know he hadn't completely broken Bernie, as there hadn't been enough time for the information to flow.

Realizing Brad would not budge on his demand, Romeo returned to Bernie. "I'll be right back, and ya had best give me the information I want." Without waiting for Bernie to respond, he turned and followed Brad out of the room. Once the door closed behind them, he said, in a low voice, "What the fuck? He be ready to tell me who be behind the bomb-making."

"I'll finish that up. You have a phone call."

Romeo stopped in his tracks. They had interrupted an interrogation for a phone call. "Ya got to be shitting me."

"Nope."

"*Merde*. It had best be the president of the fucking United States for ya to interrupt me right now."

Brad shook his head. "No. It's your mom."

Unfuckingbelievable. Why hadn't Brad just taken a message? They were seriously busy now. Yanking the portable phone Brad held out, Romeo turned away. Trying to keep his anger at Brad from showing in his voice, he took a deep breath before he answered the phone. His mom would understand. She knew he had an important job and couldn't always talk when she called. Because of that, he made sure to call her back.

"Hi, *Mamou*. Can I call ya back? I be a bit busy right now." His mind turned back to Bernie and the information he needed. The longer they let Bernie stew, the better the chance he would realize his dilemma and clam up again.

His mother wept as she spoke. "Steve, ya Papa had a heart attack. I need ya to come home."

Fear clawed at him. All thoughts of Bernie and his position at HIS disappeared from his mind. "How—" He cleared his throat. "How he be?" His father had been the epitome of health when he had last been home. Then he closed his eyes. That had been too long ago—way too long. He spoke with his mother regularly but hadn't seen her in years.

"He be fine. I just need ya to come home."

Merde. Although it was the answer he hoped to hear, he knew his mother, whose wording meant his papa was anything but fine. "I'll be there tonight." He clicked off the call, handed it back to Brad, and walked away without a backward glance. His mind spun on getting an airline ticket, getting packed, and getting the hell back to Louisiana and his family. And the woman he couldn't have but dreamed about all…the…fucking…time.

Chapter Two

DAISY MAE ROBICHOUX sprayed down the deck of *Seas the Day*, her charter boat, cursing the passengers she'd taken out earlier in the day. Why did people who got seasick allow others to push them into boating? Oh, that's right. They didn't have to clean up the vomit. She did. Or her deckhands would if they hadn't bailed.

At least the three men had a great time bringing in a nice catch, which they donated to the neighboring homeless shelter. She always recommended that option when passengers didn't want to take their catch, making them feel good about their efforts. It wasn't like they were deep-sea fishing, catching sharks. It was out in the bayou but deep enough to catch larger fish.

She shook her head at the group this morning. They hadn't had a drop to drink, but they'd been as cheerful as those who had tied one on, and she'd loved that. Until the one got sick….

"*Bonjour, Deyzee Mè*," Jean-Paul said, startling her as he walked down the dock.

"Look like a *bien amusant*," Pierre, his twin, said, laughing.

Her brothers never understood her deep attachment to the family's collection of charter boats. After their parents passed away, she and her brothers each inherited one of the three boats. JP and Pierre had sold theirs and purchased a bar. At least they had kept their father's love of John Wayne in their memories by calling the bar Dukes.

On the other hand, she didn't care if she was the only female captain at the pier. She loved the boat, the water, and even the sick people. The joy and happiness that came over someone's face when they caught a fish, especially for the first time, made this part of the job worth it. Besides, she would have to spray off the deck anyway.

Her obnoxious but loving brothers didn't ask for permission to board. They jumped on the boat, causing it to rock.

"Hey, *Sisit*," Pierre said. "We needs a favor."

Of course, they did. "*Bonjour*, JP. *Bonjour*, Pierre. *Mais non*, I appreciate the help ya offered in cleaning da *bateau*," she wisecracked.

Pierre shook his head. "Ya be the one that chose to keep this stinky mess."

JP, not to be left out, added, "*Oui*, ya could've joined us at Duke's. *Mais*, where be ya deckhands?"

The young girl she hired fell ill due to the smell of vomit. The other deckhand had called out sick. She questioned whether it was due to a hangover rather than actual suffering. He was young, and it had been a weekend trip. It wasn't the first time, but it might be the last. She would wait to see how elaborately he concocted his story.

"Whatcha want?" she asked without stopping her work. She had a deck to clean before darkness settled, making it difficult to see. She prided herself on a pristine boat—at least, as good as a charter boat could be with the wear and tear of nature's elements.

JP crossed his arms over his chest, his legs spread to withstand the rocking their boarding had caused. "We needs a favor."

She stopped spraying the deck and wiped the sweat off her forehead with a rag from her back pocket. Good grief, it had been a scorcher for May. This summer's weather didn't bode well for the South: heat, heat, and more heat. At least it wasn't a hurricane. She didn't want to deal with that turmoil all over again.

Turning, she looked at each brother. They were handsome enough with their sandy blond hair, a bit too long but not sufficient to be shaggy. Yeah, it looked good on them. They had taken after their papa. God rest his soul.

Curiosity got the better of her. "What be dis favor?"

"Ya must agree first," Pierre said.

She closed her eyes in exasperation as she shook her head. Why did they have to be so obtuse? Opening her eyes, she looked at each of them, stopping on Pierre, the oldest by six minutes. "Ya know me better than dat. Now, spill it. I no have time for dicking around."

"Language, *Sisit*," JP said, laughing. "Ya talk like a drunken sailor."

"Fuck you," she said, not caring what they said about her. They were about the only ones who drew out this type of language. "Now, spill it," she repeated, "I got no time for stupidity."

"*Oui*," Pierre said, "We"—he gestured between him and JP—"need ya to take us on a short trip. Local like."

She had previously made trips for men looking to escape it all but for her lazy-assed brothers. They hated going on the water for longer than the boat ride home since the water taxi was faster than driving. It also prevented them from getting another DUI on the roads.

She had her doubts about this trip. "What be we doing? Fishing or sightseeing?" She offered both, although the sights were few and far between. There was little in Bayou Junction, Louisiana: alligators, small islands, and abundant fish.

Returning to her brothers, maybe they were trying to butter someone up to buy into the bar or perhaps some new scheme. She knew they didn't have financial problems and wouldn't want another partner, but who knew with her brothers? Get-rich schemes, though, were the name of their game.

"Um," Pierre said, then began to fidget back and forth on his feet, looking down as he did.

What the hell? She'd never seen her brother at a loss for words. Now, her curiosity was at full tilt.

"Sightseeing," JP blurted out. "Of a sort," he mumbled at the end, but she caught it.

This sounded fishier than the smell of her passengers' last catch. "I got no time for dis," she said and turned. "Ya know my rates for a trip." She turned the hose back on, spraying another portion of her deck, waiting for their subsequent plea.

Out of her peripheral vision, she caught Pierre walking closer. She purposefully turned, with the sprayer still flowing, barely splashing him.

He jumped back and held up his hands. "*Ça va, ça va.*"

Sighing, she turned off the sprayer and gave her brothers her full attention. "What da hell be going on? I never see ya two nervous 'cept when Papa caught ya and Steve drinking his Jack."

Ah, hell. Just the mention of Steve Smith had her insides in turmoil. She had always had a crush on him, but she was his best friend's little sister. She was…. What had he called her that final night? Oh yeah, "Off limits."

She disagreed but never said anything to the contrary after he shut her down. But Steve had made his choice and got the hell out of Bayou Junction, just like he'd always said he would. Lucky bastard.

Of course, she could take her boat anywhere and start a new business. She kept the business name of Bayou Charters, which her parents had founded, just in case she bought back the other boats. That wish had not come true, but she promised herself there was always a chance to do more.

Again, she needed to catch up on what her brothers were saying. She had to stop that, but it was her bad habit for the mind to run off in another direction and lose focus when bored. And her brothers, on this occasion, bored her. She did love them, though, as only a sister could.

JP and Pierre looked at each other, and she narrowed her eyes. Something was definitely fishy with them. "Dis be another of ya get-rich schemes? A treasure map, maybe?"

They gazed at her with the same innocent looks they had perfected as teenagers while she struggled to control her emotions. Her inability to conceal her feelings often got her in trouble.

"*Non*, what make ya think dat?" JP asked.

"Well, ya be cagey as fuck right now." Again, they brought out her terrible language. She had to watch that. Her life around fishermen had taught her more than she wished to know. Word-wise, that was.

"*Mon Dieu!*" Pierre said. "We wants ta go ta a specific place *mais* needs ya secrecy."

Whatever, she decided. She always let her brothers win in the end. "What place?"

"*Bien*," JP said, "it be one of da islands. We be on land for a while, and den we needs ya to bring us home. *Mais*, keep dis quiet. We no want anyone ta know our plans."

Well, at least they were getting somewhere. Still....

"Ya know my rates. I charge by da hour."

"*Merci*," Pierre said with a broad smile on his face.

"By da way," she stopped them from leaving, "what help will ya need from me?" Should she prepare meals? Rods?

"Ta carry da treasure," JP boasted.

"*Merde*," Pierre said.

"Well, she will see da map when wes open it to find da right spot," JP whined.

"A treasure map," another masculine voice said. "*Mais oui!* How da ya two fall for dat nonsense?" Mario Xenos asked.

Daisy Mae clenched her jaw. She despised her rival charter boat owner. He'd underhandedly stolen clients from her before. Well, she thought, he could take these two boneheads. They knew the maps for Jean Lafitte's—and she'd bet her last dollar that's whose map they believed it had belonged to—were fakes.

"Dis be none of ya business, Mario," Pierre stated.

Mario raised an eyebrow in response before the twins turned and hurried away.

Her rival looked at her dirty deck and laughed. "Enjoy, *chère*," Mario said as he walked away.

Daisy Mae wanted to spray him but wouldn't be that childish with another boat owner. She despised Mario. Let him steal her brothers' trip away from her. This time, she didn't care.

Treasure map, indeed.

Chapter Three

IN THE DIM of night, Romeo navigated the familiar route to St. James Parish Hospital, a path ingrained in his memory from the countless times he and his family had driven there with his little sister before she passed away. However, at Ochsner Children's Hospital, they spent most of their time with Sally, tending to her needs and offering unwavering support. His little sister came into the world much too soon, and her fragile health presented her with a series of medical challenges. Despite her brave fight, she tragically succumbed to pneumonia at the age of eight, quietly slipping away in her sleep.

Romeo was just ten years old at the time and hadn't comprehended how a simple cold could have taken his sister's life. Now, he understood.

Striding into the hospital at a fast clip, he stepped into an elevator and punched the floor for the ICU. He was overwhelmed by memories of his family setting aside his sports activities, such as football and baseball, to accompany his sister to the hospital. Although he cared for Sally deeply, he couldn't help but resent the attention she received. At times, he even suspected that she feigned illness to disrupt his plans deliberately. Looking back, he realized that his immaturity had significantly influenced his perspective.

Romeo stepped out of the elevator and spied the nurse's station. He moved to the desk and asked, "*Bonsoir.* Would ya give me directions for Wayne Smith's room, if ya please?"

A cute nurse beamed at him. He wasn't conceited, but he knew he was an attractive man who often caught the eye of the opposite sex. But he didn't know how to handle himself in those situations. He always got tongue-tied. Hence, his pain-in-the-ass colleagues nicknamed him Romeo. He was so far from a Romeo.

"He be in da last room on da left." She pointed down the long hallway. "*Mais* someone be in there. You be family?"

He nodded. "I be his son. Is my *maman* in there?"

"She be. I let her know ya here." She smiled again and walked down the hallway—with a bit of extra sway in her step—presumably to his father's room.

A little while later, his mother emerged from the room, her eyes red and teary as she dabbed them with a tissue. Crap, she had been crying. It wasn't supposed to be a severe heart attack. Or so she had claimed, but he suspected she was not telling the truth, especially since his father was still in ICU.

When they came together, his mother fell into his embrace. Romeo always loved that he could kiss his mom on the head. The family always joked he must be the milkman's kid because he was taller than his parents. Of course, the younger generation didn't get the joke because they'd never had the milkman deliver to their homes. The delivery service stopped when he was young, but he remembered the man who had brought milk in a bottle to the house. He always got ice cream. That's how Romeo remembered him.

Romeo and his mother didn't speak, but he held her while she silently cried.

"Shh," he finally said, laying his chin on her head. "It's gonna be okay, *Mamou*." He hoped never to see the day when his mom was without his father. Together, they had married at a young age and had been inseparable ever since. He yearned to experience that kind of deep, enduring love in his own life.

After collecting herself, his mother pulled back. "They want ta watch ya papa overnight. He be stable so dey be moving him to a room."

Well, that was good news. Romeo cleared his throat, washing back his emotions. "I'd like to see him. Dat be okay?" He longed for a moment without his mother in case his father needed to impart something private.

Barbara, his mother, smiled weakly. "He'd like that."

With a solemn nod, he proceeded past her into his father's room. A wave of shock and concern engulfed him as he focused on his father, who was connected to various machines. It became apparent that the heart attack may not have been as mild as his mother had suggested.

His father opened his eyes. "*Cher*, you no need to come home for *moi*. Ya has a grand job to do."

His parents weren't impressed when he had left the FBI for Hamilton Investigation and Security. They changed their minds once he explained the type of cases HIS worked on and how their success rate was higher than the alphabets. He loved their support in his career.

Romeo smiled as best he could, considering his father could have died, and approached the bedside. "Hi, Papa. Who permitted ya to have a heart attack?" he joked. That had always been his father's question when he'd done something wrong. "Who permitted ya to…?"

Wayne chuckled and then sobered. "Hear me, Steve. We need to chat afore dey move me. I got things ta say dat I don't want ya *maman* ta hear."

Despite expecting a similar outcome, Romeo was taken aback by the overwhelming sense of pessimism and despair in the air. "*Mais oui*." He sat in the chair his mother had probably been sitting in since they'd put his father in ICU.

"*Un*, I glad ya here. Ya *maman* needs to be taken care of while I recover. How long can ya stay?"

"As long as needed," Romeo answered, knowing the Hamiltons would give him whatever time he requested. Since he began working with them, he hadn't taken a single vacation despite having abundant available time.

"*Bien. Bien.*" Wayne shifted on the bed, and Romeo stood to help. His father waved him off with a hand that had an IV in it. "I be fine."

He didn't look fine, but Romeo didn't want to argue the point. "What else?" he asked, unsure he wanted to know.

"*Deux*," his father said, "I want ya assurances dat if something happens to me, ya will care for ya *maman*."

Romeo hated that kind of talk. "Don't talk like dat, Papa. You'll be fine." There went that word again. *Fine*.

"Ya *maman* don't know dis, and ya best not tell her, but the docs says I died on dat dere table."

Romeo's heart sank like a rock to the pit of his stomach. Died? His father? He couldn't lose his father. He idolized the man.

"I jist want to know dat she be taken care of should something happen ta me. I has a little insurance policy, and da house be paid for, *mais* someone needs to be wit her. She needs someone ta care for. It's what keeps her happy."

Swallowing around the lump in his throat, Romeo would agree to anything his father asked of him. "While I expect you be living a long life, should something happen to you, I'll take care of *Mamau*."

"*Bien. Bien*," Romeo's father said again. Wayne closed his eyes, and Romeo worried he was going to sleep. "Steve," he said, then opened his eyes, "we miss ya."

Regret and sadness flooded his system. He'd stayed away way too long. All because of one thing. Well, one person. He had a thing for his best friend's sister, who was considered off-limits.

"*Trois*," his father said, "watch out for Daisy Mae—"

Romeo's heart leaped at her name, and his gut churned simultaneously.

"Her *frères*—dey be up ta something, and I think dey plan ta snare her."

How would his father know this? He attempted to ask. "How—"

"Ya *maman*. She kinda adopted Daisy Mae into our family. We know all dat go on with her and dose *frères* of hers."

Romeo's thoughts spun around Daisy Mae as part of his family. When he had left, she had been exquisitely beautiful. He couldn't help but imagine she still possessed that same timeless beauty.

Then, he recalled the night before he'd left home. Daisy Mae had snuck over to convince him to take her with him. Heck, she'd even tried to kiss him and offer up her virginity. Romeo felt the redness creep up his neck.

"What her *frères* be up to?" They'd always been into something growing up, and Romeo had been part of every adventure. He and Pierre had been best friends in school. That was, until doing what they'd all planned– getting the hell out of Bayou Junction.

"I know not. Dey be secretive 'bout it, *mais* I has a feeling it be treasure hunting 'gain."

"Treasure hunting?" he repeated as a question. They twins had always wanted to play treasure hunting when they were growing up. They still played at it?

Wayne nodded. "*Oui*. Dat be why I needs ya to keep an eye on her. Treasure hunters—dey be ruthless."

Watch over Daisy Mae? Would he still have feelings for her? Oh, how he'd wanted to take her up on her offer the night before he'd left town. But she was part of the reason he'd been going.

What was she like now? Those questions and more ran through his mind. He knew he should turn tail and run, but he couldn't let something happen to her. "I'll watch her." *And those damn brothers of hers,* he secretly promised.

The good news was that Pierre wasn't his best friend anymore. That meant Daisy Mae wasn't his best friend's sister. He couldn't decide if that was good or bad. All he knew was that he craved to see her. He hoped she was married with ten kids by now so he could easily walk away this time.

"I needs sleep," his father told him. "Glad ya be home."

Romeo nodded, stood, walked to the door, and stopped, turning to his tired-looking father. "I've missed ya too, Papa." He had missed his parents, but with video chat, it was like he was home. However, Romeo didn't have to hide his feelings for Daisy Mae.

Seeing the smile on his father's face, Romeo exited the room, intent on finding his mother so they could chat. He knew she'd be a mess of worry. And from what his father had said, she had every right to be in such a state.

Had he really almost lost his father? Without spending time with him lately? Romeo's heart broke at the thought of his father dying on the table during his heart attack. He wasn't ready to lose a parent. Then again, who was?

Deep in thought, Romeo approached the ICU waiting room, not paying much attention. His step faltered as he closed on his mother, and his heart leaped. A woman sat holding his mother's hand, whispering to Barbara. Even with some of the woman's hair shadowing her face while she bent down to his mother, Romeo knew the woman. He'd craved her for years. He thought he'd finally let her go in his heart, but the way it beat now, he knew that to be a lie.

He wondered what kind of trouble her brothers were getting her into. Romeo didn't want her embroiled in one of their schemes. Yeah, his mom had kept him updated on his old friends and their antics. In his mind, they'd turned into nothing but trouble.

He continued walking to his mother, his eyes on Daisy Mae. Would she recognize him like he'd recognized her? Indeed, he hadn't changed as much as she had.

The women stood as he approached. He couldn't keep his eyes off Daisy Mae. In his peripheral, he saw his mother wipe the tears from her eyes with a tissue. Romeo couldn't stop staring into the bright blue eyes of his old love. Old? He mentally laughed at himself. With the way his body came alive with her around, he expected her to still be the one he loved. Maybe now they could have a shot. She wasn't the bumbling teenager following him and her brothers and trying to play with them. No, this Daisy Mae was all woman in her shorts with tanned legs, a T-shirt showcasing what he assumed was her charter service and the ever-present baseball cap in her hand.

"How he be?" Barbara asked.

Romeo never took his eyes off Daisy Mae's. "He be resting." He needed to say hello to Daisy Mae, but, as usual, his tongue got tied around a beautiful woman. It hadn't been that way when they'd been growing up. At least, only when he'd realized he liked her more than a friend.

"Steve, ya 'member Daisy Mae?"

His heart wanted to scream, "*Oui!* I thought about her often," but his mind shut down. So, he nodded.

Daisy Mae's jaw tightened. "It 'bout time ya came home."

Taken aback by the venom in her voice, Romeo grappled for a suitable response. "Hi" was all that came out. He wanted to slap himself on the forehead. "Hi," was all he could say. This was Daisy Mae. He didn't want her to see him as a bumbling fool now that he was older. He knew he could talk around her, so why had he clammed up?

Narrowing her eyes, Daisy Mae put her ballcap on her head and turned to Barbara. "I gotta go. Please keep me updated." She turned and left without another word or glance to Romeo.

Watching her walk away with her magnificent ass, Romeo wondered what the hell had just happened between them?

Chapter Four

DAISY MAE REMOVED her baseball cap, revealing a mop of unruly blonde hair. With deft fingers, she carefully threaded her tousled locks through the small back loop of the cap. After securing her hair, she firmly replaced the cap on her head, the worn fabric feeling familiar against her fingertips. She knew he would eventually return. How could he not when his father had a heart attack? Well, he'd waited way too long to return. She was over him.

Her anger stemmed from the pain of his constant absence, which caused his mother great emotional distress. Yes, that was it.

Groaning at the lie she told herself, she started her pickup truck and left the hospital parking lot. If things worked out, she wouldn't have to run into him again. She didn't need to visit Barbara while he was in town. Barbara would have enough on her hands with her husband's health and her son's return.

Daisy Mae gazed off into the distance, her mind swirling with questions about the duration of his visit and the last time she'd seen him. Embarrassment flooded her system. She'd thrown herself at him to keep him from leaving or that he should consider taking her with him. That turned out beautifully. He'd left without a thought to her, and she'd remained stuck in their small town.

Realizing Steve would dominate her thoughts, she turned the truck toward her friend's house. At least there, she could talk it out. Shelly Tibidoux had been her friend since preschool. Her only problem with Shelly was that Shelly had asked Steve to Prom, and he'd said yes.

Daisy Mae had yearned to muster the courage to ask him, but her nerves always eluded her. She and Shelly hadn't spoken for almost a year back then. Still, Daisy Mae hadn't tossed away their friendship over that since they'd been teenagers then, and Steve hadn't made any advances toward Shelly at Prom—not even a quick peck goodnight.

To avoid her thoughts on the long drive, Daisy Mae turned on the radio to her favorite country station. After a while, she turned the system off. She couldn't listen to one more sad love song when her life had turned to epitomize one.

When her phone rang, she welcomed the distraction. Pushing the hands-free button on her steering wheel to answer the call, she tried to sound happy to hear from her brother. "*Bonsoir*, Pierre."

"We like ta go out tomorrow."

No "*Bonsoir, Sisit*" or "How you be, *Deyzee Mè*?" It irritated her that they ignored her feelings, not that she shared her feelings with the two of them either.

Now that her plan to stay with Barbara at the hospital had been shot to hell, she decided to accommodate her brothers. Besides, she needed the distraction, and a useless treasure hunt would do it. "Dat be fine. I launch at *huit* wit or without ya." She clicked the button to end the call.

Thinking about tomorrow, she smiled. She hadn't told Pierre that he and JP would act as her crew since she'd given her team the day off. Besides, they wanted to be secretive, which gave them the opportunity. However, her lazy brothers would surely protest.

Pulling into Shelly's drive, Daisy Mae realized she should have called first. With all the vehicles, it appeared Shelly had a class in the yoga studio attached to the house. Tapping her fingers on the steering wheel, Daisy Mae decided to wait. This was too important.

Pulling up to the building, she noticed a group dressed in comfortable yoga attire exiting. She let out a sigh of relief and thought, *Thank goodness*. After Shelly, who owned the studio, waved the last person out, Daisy Mae exited her truck and approached the entrance.

As usual, Shelly was all smiles. "*Bonsoir, mon ami*. What brings ya out tonight?"

"He be back," Daisy Mae shot out.

Quizzically, Shelly looked at her. "Who?" Then, as if remembering some secret, her expressive eyes widened. "You no mean—"

"*Oui*. Steve be here."

"Help me straighten da studio. I'll call da girls. We'll have dem pick up ice cream."

Ice cream sounded divine, but Shelly wouldn't eat any. As a health food nut, she ate plant-based foods, and the ice cream Daisy Mae and their friends ate was definitely not plant-based, although they undoubtedly had some substitute for it.

As the two women tidied up the studio, their friends arrived. Alice Fournier and her sister Marie joined them as they walked along the stone path to the home's entrance. Once inside, Alice took a pint of chocolate brownie fudge ice cream and gave it to Daisy Mae. Shelly handed her a spoon.

Daisy Mae flopped onto the plush couch and wasted no time opening the ice cream. While the others were still juggling their pints, she dug in without bothering with a bowl. She believed that a woman nursing a broken heart could only find solace in scoops of ice cream straight from the tub. Perhaps it was an unspoken golden rule, or maybe it was just an instinctual craving for comfort.

Making herself a disgusting-looking, plant-based, post-workout shake, Shelly asked, "How he look?"

Daisy Mae hesitated, the spoon poised near her lips, as she contemplated Shelly's potential pursuit of him again. With her single status and striking beauty, Shelly overshadowed Daisy Mae. While Shelly embodied undeniable femininity, Daisy Mae projected the image of a seasoned charter boat captain, often seen sporting a baseball cap. It was common for the men to favor Shelly over Daisy Mae whenever they gathered at the bar. It seemed that Daisy Mae's grown tomboy persona failed to capture their attention. Which generally worked for her.

"*Bon.*" Romeo looked incredibly delicious. He exuded a rugged charm in his well-fitted black cargo pants, snug black T-shirt, and sturdy combat boots. His attire perfectly suited her image of him at his job in Maryland. She couldn't help but wonder whether he had rushed over directly from work or had any other clothing. Given his youth penchant for cargo shorts and T-shirts, his current outfit choice wasn't far from what she remembered.

Alice shook her head, pointed to Daisy Mae's socks with a spoon, and laughed. "Why you no get a cat already?"

Daisy Mae wore cat socks because she loved cats. "Cats no like da water, and I be on da water too often."

Shaking her head, Marie took another bite of ice cream. After swallowing, she said, "I see cats on da water on dat social media. Ya just have ta find da right one."

"And how, oh wise one, do ya recommend I do dat? Ask the shelter for a tryout of each cat ta see who no go berserk aboard the *bateau*?"

"Why not? Dey might even know which cats no be afraid of water."

"Okay, so da cat no be afraid of water. Exactly how da ya 'xpect me to keep it away from da client's catch of da day?" Daisy Mae saw a fluffy cat trying to drag off a largemouth bass. She giggled at the thought. The others must have also because they all burst into laughter.

Sobering, Shelly stated matter-of-factly, "Train da cat."

"Train it?" Daisy Mae sputtered. "Do ya even know da first thing 'bout cats?" Then she shook her head. "Why we be talking 'bout this? I be having a more serious problem."

Shelly drank her shake and raised her eyebrows at Daisy Mae. "*Oui*, ya do. Do ya still love him?"

"*Non*," Daisy Mae blurted, knowing it was a lie. Yet, how could she love him when he didn't love her back? Why did life have to be so cruel?

Shelly smiled and winked. "Good. Maybe I go for him den."

Daisy Mae could have punched her friend until she realized the woman was joking to rile her. And Shelly had succeeded. Daisy Mae put the spoon down on the ice cream lid on the coffee table. "*Oui*, so I do. But it be one-sided, so what does it matter?"

Marie pointed her spoon at her. "It matters a lot if it be bothering ya."

"*Mais non*," Daisy Mae retorted, "he went to college, den FBI, and den take dat job up North. He no visit his family. He calls his mother on da video to keep her happy. It like he no want to come home."

Once, she thought her love for Steve Smith was a childhood infatuation. Yet, as a teenager, it grew more profound. She knew it was more than that when he came home after graduating college. And he didn't seem to notice or care. He and her brothers, mostly Pierre, would hang out and exclude her.

At first, she thought because of how she'd thrown herself at him, but later, she realized he didn't care for her at all.

Daisy Mae adjusted her ballcap. "He probably be embarrassed. We still be a bit of a backwoods parish."

Alice smiled. "Dat we be, *mais,* we love it."

Nodding, Daisy Mae agreed.

"Tell me, how be ya *frerés*?" Alice, a sheriff's deputy, asked with a twinkle in her eyes.

Knowing Alice had a crush on one of her brothers, although Daisy Mae couldn't guess which one since Alice always asked about them both, Daisy Mae smiled. "They be up to mischief again."

The ladies laughed as if that wasn't an oddity with her brothers.

Patting her flat belly, Marie asked, "When dey not be? What it be dis time?"

She spilled the truth with her friends, not caring about her brothers' desire to keep it a secret. "Treasure hunting. *Mais*," Daisy explained, "they gots a new treasure map."

"Which one dey be looking for?" Shelly gathered the spoons and picked up all the ice cream cartons. "Jean Lafitte's or da Bonafice Plantation treasure?"

"I know not where we be going. *Mais*, didn't someone find da Bonafice Plantation treasure already?"

"I think so. Be right back." Shelly stood and returned to the kitchen with the ice cream and spoons.

Reentering the room, Shelly said, "Wow. It be sounding mysterious." She sat at the other end of the couch, leaned back, and put her feet on the coffee table, crossing them, showcasing her " "Yoga is my life" socks.

"It definitely be."

Alice startled Daisy Mae with, "*Mon Dieu!* Dey stole it."

"What ya be talking about?" Daisy Mae asked. Her brothers were many things, but not thieves. At least, she didn't think so. She prayed not.

"Antione Rousseau, in da next parish—"

Daisy Mae waved her on. "*Oui*, we knows who he be." Who didn't? He was the wealthiest treasure hunter in these parts. He'd made his fortune on Jean Lafitte's smaller treasures.

"Well," Alice continued, "I read a report dat someone had broken into his home and stolen a map. One he reported as authentic."

Daisy Mae's hand flew to her mouth. *Mais non!* Could her brothers have done it? No. She trusted her brothers had a few morals. "Somehow, I doubt dis map be authentic. It probably be another money scheme someone has sold dem."

"I hope so," Alice said, all sheriff's deputy.

Changing the subject, Marie asked, "Do ya need an extra hand? I be free tomorrow."

Daisy Mae considered it. Marie, a part-time bartender at Duke's, was a good deckhand. She knew how to throw ropes, tie up the boat, and all the other tasks the captain couldn't do while steering. "I'd love to have ya come, but me brothers said only da *trois* of us."

"Do ya brothers realize they be deckhands on da *bateau*?"

The four women looked at each other and busted out laughing. They knew how lazy JP and Pierre were.

"*Mais*," Shelly said, "ya have to let me know how it goes."

Daisy Mae nodded. "*Mais oui! Mais*," she smiled, "I could be calling ya to bail me out of jail for strangling *mon frères*, me."

"Okay," Alice said, changing the subject away from the law, "let's get to ya real problem."

Leaning back like Shelly, Daisy Mae crossed her feet on the table. "I no want to care 'bout him like I do, but I no can help it."

"Ya need a man who can spark ya interest and distract ya from Steve, who, by da way, left our parish without a backward glance."

"It's not like I told him I loved him," Daisy Mae said. "He didn't know when he left." This wasn't true, but Daisy Mae had never told a soul about that night before Steve left. How would she have endured the shame?

"*Chère*," Shelly said, "ya were his best friend's sister, and Steve is full of southern honor. *Mais oui*, he wouldn't have gone after ya." Shelly tilted her head and grinned. "Now, though, dey no be best friends, do dey?"

"When he come home from da college, he all but ignored me. He and Pierre weren't close den."

Alice scratched her head. "Maybe it's time ya told him ya love him."

Daisy Mae dropped her feet off the coffee table and leaned forward. "Have ya lost your ever-loving mind?" The last time was still fresh in her mind, even though it'd been years. That hadn't worked, so what would make her think it'd work now?

Alice smiled and nodded. "Possible. But it would help move tings forward. There's no telling how long he be here dis time."

Daisy Mae dropped her shoulders and sighed. "It do matter. I still be angry at him. Plus, I won't leave here and da family business. Steve couldn't get out of here fast enough."

"Well then, what are ya going to do? Dis may be ya only chance."

Daisy Mae realized that but knew it wouldn't work in the end. She wanted to remain here and rebuild the family business. Daisy Mae chose to be on the water instead of at home waiting for her husband to return from work.

"I be avoiding him and eventually find someone who heals me broken heart. And I will help find a treasure and put me business back on da map." Now, if it all worked out like Daisy Mae wanted, she'd be completely and utterly surprised. However, she had hope, which had gotten her far. Deep inside, Daisy Mae still hoped that

Steve would declare his undying love for her. Knowing that wouldn't happen, she had to focus realistically.

Treasure hunt, it was.

Chapter Five

LATER THAT EVENING, Brad Hamilton, taking the time to inquire, spoke to Romeo on the phone and asked, "How is your dad doing?"

Romeo felt a surge of fear as he imagined his father dying on the operating table. "He be better." Anything was better than dead. Thank goodness he'd been rushed to the hospital in time.

"How long do you need?"

Thinking of what his dad had said about his mom and Daisy Mae, he had no fucking idea. "I have no ETA."

"Not a problem. Bravo Team is due a break. Jake and Alpha Team are spinning up for a new op now," Brad informed him.

Romeo, Bravo Team's second in command, was hopeful that the scheduled time off was not due to any shortcomings on his part. Considering the team's recent busy schedule, everyone seemed to be looking forward to the well-deserved break. "*Merci, cher.*"

"No problem."

With Romeo's thoughts on HIS, he asked, "How did da interrogation end? Did Bernie spill his guts?"

Brad cleared his throat, signaling that he was about to give a non-answer. "Don't worry about things here," he reassured Romeo, his tone steady. "We've got things covered." With that, he ended the call, leaving Romeo with a sense of lingering curiosity, yet no opportunity to press for further details.

Romeo stared at his cell as if it held the answer to his other concern: How would he discover what was going on to alleviate his dad's worries?

There seemed to be no way around it. He would have to visit the twins. Not that it was a bad idea. He had drifted apart from them after he left for college. Pierre had accused him of being too uppity to spend time with backwoods folk, which was why he didn't come home. If only Pierre knew the truth.

He checked the time and decided that a late dinner at Duke's was in order. He grabbed his wallet, his dad's truck keys, and backup weapon–tucking it in the ankle holster–and headed out. He desired to carry his primary gun but didn't need to bring attention to it or him. Even though Louisiana was a reciprocal state, Maryland didn't have an agreement with them, so Louisiana wouldn't honor his permit to conceal carry. He didn't consider the backup weapon a problem. It was out of sight and would hopefully go unnoticed. If not, he'd call Brad to bail him out of jail.

Driving through town, if one could call it that, with the sparse buildings, memories ran through his mind. He and the twins, especially he and Pierre, had done things that embarrassed him now. They'd been basically juvenile delinquents. Not completely jail-worthy, but a time or two, they'd hit dark gray areas. Like when they TP'd the English teacher's home. She never approved of their Cajun French. But that was what they'd learned since birth.

Romeo had almost lost his Cajun French language skills after attending college, yet he still unconsciously used a few words, especially when he returned home.

Pulling into Duke's dirt parking lot, Romeo smiled. He recalled the numerous attempts he and the twins tried to use fake IDs here to get served, but they never worked. It had been foolish to try repeatedly with different IDs.

Now, the twins owned the place. How apropos.

Romeo pulled down his ball cap, opened the door of his father's truck, and exited. He wondered if he'd run into Daisy Mae inside. His gut clenched at the thought. Boy, was she pissed at him. Why exactly? He wasn't sure. It wasn't like he dated her and walked away. He'd never have done that to her, of all people. But was it still because he wouldn't take her with him when he'd left? Or that he wouldn't take *her* before he left? *What should I do now?*

He didn't want to contemplate that now. As his dad worried, he needed to find out what the hell was going on and if Daisy Mae was really in trouble.

Entering the bar, Romeo slowly scanned the space, left to right. It certainly hadn't changed much. Peanuts were still on the ground, and there was a fabulous view over the water.

"*Bonsoir, cher!*" JP shouted from behind the bar.

Smiling, Romeo walked forward to shake his friend's hand. He looked around for Pierre and saw him sitting at the end of the bar.

"*Bonsoir*. I hear congratulations be in order," Romeo told JP as they shook hands. "I heard you *deux* bought this pub."

"It coulda been da *trois* of us," Pierre grumpily said from a barstool.

Romeo moved to a seat beside his old best friend. "Now, I know better than dat, Pierre. Ya *deux* always had plans to buy dis place so ya could get a drink anytime ya wanted."

"And ya always had plans to leave dis place," Pierre spat out.

So, it was like that. "Ya knew I wanted to be FBI, *mon ami*."

Pierre leisurely took a sip from the tall, frosty beer glass before him. Meanwhile, Romeo caught the attention of JP, who was tending the bar, as he motioned for a drink for himself.

"So," Romeo said once he sipped the homebrew, "what's been happening?"

"*Beaucoup*," Pierre said curtly.

Romeo wanted to smack Pierre and his snappishness. "Do we need to go a few rounds and work dis out, Pierre? Ya know I can still take ya."

"Maybe we should," Pierre responded.

JP turned to his brother. "*Mon frère,* git over it. Steve left, but he be here now. Let's take him ta help tomorrow."

Pierre shook his head. "*Non*. No fucking way, *cher*."

Intrigued, Romeo asked casually, "Take me where? I be bored. I can go."

"*Mais non*," Pierre repeated vehemently.

Romeo turned to Pierre. "As your *frerè* said, get da fuck over it. I be here now. Can't we make da best of it?"

"You be leaving 'gain." Pierre drank and slammed down his empty glass.

"*Mais oui*. I have a job in Maryland."

"Dat's it," Pierre said, pulling back his shoulders and thrusting his thumb to point to the door. "Outside."

Great. Romeo hadn't found himself in a raucous bar brawl since Grits dragged them into trouble down in Mexico. Reflecting on the adrenaline-fueled and perilous altercation, Romeo couldn't help but shake his head, hoping fervently that he wouldn't have to repeat that chaotic night.

Romeo downed the last of his beer, the bitter taste lingering on his tongue as he pushed the empty glass away. "Let's do it," he declared with a grim determination, his fists clenched with a strong desire to punch Pierre in the jaw. He led the way toward the front door and into the dark, nearly empty parking lot.

As Romeo pivoted, JP threw a forceful punch that landed squarely on his jaw. Agonizing pain surged through the side of Romeo's face. *Son of a bitch.*

Rubbing his jaw and acting like it hadn't hurt like a punch from a pro, Romeo said, "Is dat all ya got?"

Pierre's face reddened, and he took another swing at Romeo. This time, Romeo was prepared and easily side-stepped the punch. In return, he jabbed Pierre in the gut.

When his friend doubled over in pain, clenching his stomach, Romeo asked, "Enough?"

With a menacing growl, Pierre lunged forward, leading with his head and landing a solid blow to Romeo's gut. The impact knocked the wind out of Romeo, sending both crashing to the ground. Reacting swiftly, Romeo pushed Pierre off him and scrambled to his feet before Pierre could regain his bearings. They eyed each other warily, circling as tension hung heavy in the air.

"What da fuck be your problem? Why can't ya act like a grown-up and get over shit?" Romeo asked.

"Ya broke her heart," Pierre spat.

Confused at that statement, Romeo asked, "Whose heart?"

"Ya know, *couyon*. She loved ya, and ya ignored her, then left when she be old enough to date."

Was he talking about Daisy Mae? Surely not. Pierre would never have approved. "Shelly and I had nothing in common. It was just Prom."

Pierre rushed in with a gut punch, and Romeo stepped back. Pierre lost his balance and almost fell. It allowed Romeo to encircle Pierre's neck from behind.

Holding the man tight around the neck and his left arm behind his back, Romeo asked in a low voice, meant for only Pierre. "What da fuck you be ranting on about?"

"*Deyzee Mè*," Pierre grunted out.

"Dude, she be ya sister. You always told me she be off-limits."

"Well, ya shoulda asked."

"Look, I'm not going to fight you over ya sister. She be a grown woman, and I be a grown man. If we hit it off, *bien*. Suppose we don't, *bien*. It no longer be ya concern." Romeo released Pierre and pushed the man forward.

"*Mon Dieu!*" Romeo said, "Can we start over?"

Pierre hesitated, rubbing his neck before finally extending his hand. "Welcome home, *mon ami*."

Unsure if it was a trick, Romeo narrowed his eyes and watched Pierre as they shook hands. "Glad to be back. Can we return inside and have a cold one if we be done?" Romeo dusted the dirt off his clothing from the tumble to the ground.

Instantly changed, as only Pierre could do, his friend smiled. "It be on me." Pierre confidently guided the group back inside to where JP waited, accompanied by a small crowd of eager spectators who had gathered to witness the fight.

Romeo stood for a moment, absorbing what Pierre had said. She'd loved him. Could that have been true? Sure, she'd said as much before he left, but he figured she was trying to get him to take her with him. Besides, she'd been sixteen. What had she known about love?

It probably wouldn't have worked. Not with the life he'd led. Lots of undercover operations with the FBI and lots of missions with HIS. She'd have hated being home alone.

His mind wondered. What about now? Did she still love him? Did he love her? Then he mentally shook his head. What did it matter? He was here for his mom and dad. And right now, his dad needed him to keep an eye on the twins and Daisy Mae, and that's what he'd do.

Once they sat at the bar again, JP set three beer glasses before them. He raised his glass. "May ya live all da days of ya life."

They raised their glasses and drank deeply.

"*Mais oui*," Pierre said, "we could use ya help."

And like that, it was like he'd never left.

Chapter Six

DAISY MAE ANXIOUSLY scanned the horizon, hoping to catch sight of her tardy brothers. The boat was ready; she had fueled herself with a gallon of strong coffee, and breakfast had been hastily consumed. Despite all her preparations, they were nowhere to be seen. Frustration crept in as she acknowledged that if they didn't arrive within the next fifteen minutes, she would have to abandon their plans for the day. Daisy had pressing matters to attend to—repairs awaited her at the old homestead, tasks that she could no longer put off.

Daisy Mae inherited her parents' home upon their passing. It was almost one hundred years old and always needed something repaired or updated. But she loved the place and the memories.

"*Bonjour!*" JP said as he and Pierre approached.

Merde. She was itching to know the truth about the map from them.

Once the two men boarded, Daisy Mae couldn't wait, so she exclaimed, "Did ya steal dat map?" She wouldn't take them out if they turned out to be the missing map. Daisy Mae didn't need that kind of trouble coming down on her. She'd heard how ruthless Antoine Rousseau was. Who hadn't in this neck of the woods? Treasure hunters around the world feared him. From what Daisy Mae had heard, you never crossed the man. That is if you wanted to live.

The twins looked at each other and then at her. Their innocent personas didn't fool her. They may not have stolen the map, but they were up to something.

"*Mais non!*" Pierre assured her. "We bought it."

"We did," JP echoed.

"Hmph." She didn't know whether to believe them or not. Since they had no reason to lie to her, she'd have to accept cautiously. "Stow ya gear and grab those tow lines," she instructed as she moved to start the boat.

Pierre tossed his gear on the floor, saying, "We be waiting on another."

Who on earth would they want with them treasure hunting? She knew everyone in town was an amateur treasure hunter, but for the twins to share that seemed all kinds of wrong.

"Here he come," Pierre said, tossing his gear near his brothers.

What part of stowing their gear did they not understand? They just put it in the way. "Move ya gear," Daisy Mae said before she looked down the pier.

Mais non! She did not want to see or speak to this man. He'd ripped her heart out and walked away without looking back. She would not give him a second chance to make a fool of her. How could her brothers want him along, of all people?

"Grab the lines. Ya man, he be late."

"*Dayzee Mè,*" Pierre pleaded, "wait for him."

"*Non*," she asserted. "He no step foot on me *bateau*."

"Why not?" she heard in that deep, sexy voice. Romeo hadn't stepped aboard but waited for permission on the dock. At least someone respected courtesies.

Because my heart can't take ya rejection, again. "I have no use for ya, Steve. You not welcome 'round me, especially on my *Seas*."

Steve raised his eyebrows. "*Mais*, why not?"

Why couldn't Steve understand he be slowly killing me? She didn't want to be the bitch, but it was the only way to harden her heart against him. If they tried to be friends again, she'd crumble and be left in the dust again. Alone.

Daisy Mae huffed and put her hands on her hips. "Because I be da captain, and I say so."

"All right, little rocket," Steve said and winked. "We play it ya way."

That was a new nickname, but she wanted to avoid starting a dialogue by asking him what it meant.

"Sorry, *mon amis*," Steve told her brothers. "I guess I won't join ya today."

"*Dayzee Mè*," Pierre said, now in her face, "let him onboard. He be going to help us. He be da crew."

Daisy Mae narrowed her eyes at Pierre. "You and JP be my crew."

JP shook his head. "No, we hired him to be da crew. So, ya need to allow him onboard."

Merde. Those lazy brothers of hers had hired someone to work for them. She should have guessed they'd do something like that. But she'd never imagined Steve would be the help. Didn't he already have a job?

Mon Dieu! Daisy Mae pondered whether he had given up his job in the north to live closer to his parents. The thought of constantly having him around in the same town was overwhelming. She would have to expedite her plans to relocate to a bigger town. Fortunately, she had enough savings to make the move.

Pierre approached her and grinned. "Put on ya big girl panties and let him board. I know not why ya deny him. He be done nothing wrong."

Daisy Mae could see she'd never win this battle. So, she said, "Get your ass on board, stow all da gear properly, and grab da lines." With that, she spun on her heels and prepared to launch. *Men*, they were the bane of her existence.

With a chuckle, Steve stepped on *Seas the Day* and shook her brothers' hands. Then, he gave her a mock salute and grabbed the twins' gear from the bottom of the boat to stow appropriately. After emerging from below, he held one line and then the other, loosening them from the pier.

Merde. Daisy Mae had been so focused on keeping Steve away that she'd forgotten to review the map JP had in his hand. "I need me some direction, if you please."

"Just head south," Pierre instructed. "We tells ya when to turn."

Daisy Mae didn't operate like that. She wanted to know where she would be traversing the waters. "Give me da damn map," she demanded. "I needs to see da waterways before ya drive us somewhere we get the *bateau* stuck."

She knew they wouldn't do that. The twins were also good captains of these waterways, but she wanted to know what they had.

JP approached and unrolled the map on the dash in front of her. He pointed to a spot on the map. "We be going to dis island," he said.

Thinking, Daisy Mae scrunched up her brows. She traced their path and shook her head. "There be no island dere." She remembered going in that direction before. There'd been no island.

"Trust me," Pierre said, "it be dere."

It was their dime to waste because they'd brought *him* along. Thinking of Steve, she turned to see where he stood. Daisy Mae jumped, and her heart rate leaped. Steve stood right behind her. When had he become silent?

"I have my doubts also," Steve added.

Whoopdefuckingdo. He hadn't been here in years and surely didn't remember all the waterways and islands.

Daisy Mae tried hard to ignore Steve and turned back to her brothers. "Your crew member, he be crowding me. Have him polish something." Sure, it was petty, but she didn't know how else to act around Steve. Where did they stand? They'd never been a couple—even though she'd tried. He had to have known she'd loved him. How couldn't he have the way she'd offered herself up to him to be her first and only? And, he'd left, left her.

"I be right here," Steve said. "Ya could speak to me, little rocket."

Daisy Mae wanted to grit her teeth at the smooth voice. Since when had Steve become confident around women? He'd always been scared to speak with a woman. She reminded herself that he'd only been tongue-tied around her near the end.

"Why do dey call ya Romeo?" Daisy Mae asked, thinking of how Barbara had laughed at it with her.

"*Merde*. I'll go polish something," Steve responded.

Touchy, she decided. Well, she always had something to run him off with. She'd put that in her pocket for another time.

"You go do dat." Daisy Mae wanted to turn around and get one more glance at Steve in that tight T-shirt that showed off the muscles he'd perfected since leaving home. Plus, she could tell he had new tattoos she craved to trace along his arms. But she wouldn't. She wouldn't get all googly-eyed over him again.

Pierre frowned at her. "What be wit ya and Steve? You liked him—*beaucoup*."

"It not ya business," she said. "Tell me about dis treasure ya be hunting."

Excitedly, JP told her of one of Jean Lafitte's little-known treasures hidden in the islands. Her brother believed the map was proper, but she had doubts. Authentic maps were few and far between. However, this map did look ancient with its faded print and falling apart at the edges. Forgery or not, it would easily fool suspecting prey.

"So, what be me cut?" she asked to keep the conversation going. She didn't want Steve to reappear and suddenly attempt to speak with her.

JP fidgeted. "Uh."

"Uh, what?" Daisy Mae asked. "*Mais*, let me guess, ya no plan ta give me a share. Don't you know da captain always gets a cut of da booty?"

This conversation was moot since she didn't expect them to find a treasure, but she liked how it affected her brothers.

"Who pissed in ya cereal dis morning?" Pierre asked.

Okay, so she was acting like a bitch. That wasn't her. Daisy Mae wouldn't allow Steve's presence to turn her into one. "*Mais*, I be sorry," she said to her brothers. "I be tired, is all." She was tired. The women had stayed up late watching movies and enjoying the company. It was rare that everyone had the same time off work.

"And wit Steve?" Pierre asked.

"That be different," Daisy Mae said. "*Mais*, I'll be nicer." It'd be challenging to harden her heart against Steve if she had to be pleasant. But she was a big girl and could do anything she set her mind to doing.

"That be all we ask," Pierre said before ushering JP away. Through her peripheral, she saw them join Steve aft of the boat. The twins opened a cooler near the benches lining the ship's rear. Sure enough, they brought out beer. It wasn't even nine in the morning, and they were already drinking. Figures.

Then, she noticed Steve grabbing water. Well, some things had changed. She wondered what had changed with Steve and couldn't decide whether to find out.

So, she kept her gaze forward and focused on finding the non-existent island her brothers swore existed. Steve, it would be best to ignore him for now.

Unfortunately, her heart didn't want to ignore him. She'd take that as a small win if only her heart would stop fluttering at his presence.

Chapter Seven

STEVE GRINNED AT the transformation of a spitting-mad Daisy Mae to a pleasant boat captain. He liked her being nice to him, but she looked sexy when angry as she put her hands on her hips or pulled her ballcap down low and mumbled to herself.

Why had he not spoken with her about his desire when he came home from college? Maybe because he knew he wouldn't stay. Of course, he could have asked. Perhaps she'd have still cared for him. *Couyon.*

The breeze off the water felt unique and refreshing on his face. The old times came back to him. When he and the twins would take out a boat to fish and drink, they weren't old enough to drink and had stolen it from their parents, but hey, it'd been fun. Steve mentally shook his head. They'd never fooled their parents, especially when he or a twin would come home and throw up the evidence.

Pierre looked at Steve. "What did ya do to piss her off?"

Shrugging, Steve pulled his ballcap off and reset it on his head. He sure wished to hell he knew. "Couldn't tell ya."

"Well," Pierre said, "fix it, *mais* she be taking it out on us."

The twins walked away from him to their sister. Steve watched the three look over a piece of what appeared to be parchment—presumably the map, which he doubted was the real thing. There was this unknown island, and there was a treasure. Steve kept his mouth shut about it all.

Giving up being alone on the boat, he walked to the others. The twins quickly grabbed the map—like he wouldn't know where they were going. And Daisy Mae glanced at him, then away.

It was hard to believe what Pierre had told him about Daisy Mae loving him. She'd always been there, but he'd taken her jumping at him before he left as her chance to go, not really be with him.

The hair on the back of Steve's neck prickled, and he looked around. The water appeared clear in all directions, and no other boats were in sight. *Mais*…. "Hand me the binoculars," he said, wanting to look at a glint he'd briefly seen.

Daisy Mae only raised her brows at him as if he'd asked for control of her boat.

Instinct had Steve grab the binoculars and search the area behind them. Yes, he'd felt the presence of another boat.

Behind him, Daisy Mae asked, "What it be?"

Without turning, Steve answered, "Another *bateau*."

Pierre snatched the binoculars from Steve. "Let me see." After a moment, he said, "*Merde*, we be followed."

"*Merde*," Daisy Mae said and shook her head. "This be a big pond, and we not the only *bateau* to float it, so don't get all paranoid on me. It just be another *bateau* out for a tour or fishing."

Pierre grumbled. "I know not. Maybe we go a different route."

Steve watched Daisy Mae close her eyes, and her lips moved as if counting to ten. Something inside him flared to life as he remembered teaching her that the twins would tease her when she was young.

An young, crying Daisy Mae stood in the backyard, breaking Steve's teenage heart. "It's okay," he'd said, "you must ignore ya brothers when dey be behaving like dat. It be giving dem da power ta do it more often."

"Mais, mais," she repeated, "dey made fun of me hair."

Steve didn't have the heart to tell her it looked pretty interesting with pink stripes, but it was still Daisy Mae. "Try dis when dey makes fun of ya."

She stopped crying and sniffed. "Que?" She looked wide-eyed like he was about to tell her a secret.

"Here's what I want ya to do. I want ya to close ya eyes."

"Okay." She tightly closed her eyes.

"Relax," he encouraged.

She did. "Dis not work."

"We not be done. Okay, silently count to dix and focus on your breathing. Don't think 'bout ya brothers. Think 'bout being on da water," he'd added, knowing that was her favorite spot.

She did as he asked and opened her eyes. Then, she surprised him by throwing her arms around him. "Merci, Steve. Merci beaucoup. I feels much better."

Steve had to push her away before she felt his pants tighten on him. He was a teenager, and control still didn't exist. "Okay," he said at arm's length, "try dat whenever ya need to control ya temper or deal wit da twins."

Daisy Mae swung her hand to her right hip and narrowed her eyes at him. "I no have a temper," she said.

"We not be taking a different route." Daisy Mae's words brought him from his memories. He agreed with her since he didn't believe there was a treasure. However, his gut was telling him to be wary of other travelers near them. He knew the mention of a treasure sent people into stupid mode.

"They follow us," Pierre insisted.

"*Mais non!*" Daisy Mae argued.

JP, the peacemaker, said, "Since it be our dime, will ya at least humor us and take an indirect route?"

After a moment, Daisy Mae turned the boat. "Okay, but 'member, ya said it was ya dime."

Steve wanted to laugh when Pierre punched JP on the shoulder. "What da fuck?" Pierre asked his brother.

"*Mais*, it will be," JP said, "when we finds da treasure."

Steve was glad Daisy Mae hadn't heard that.

He went below to explore. Grabbing water from the fridge, he familiarized himself with the below deck before returning to the stairs. Daisy Mae had done well for herself. He knew this had been one of the fleet boats from her family, but she'd kept it up well.

Back on deck, he went to Daisy Mae and stood behind her.

Without looking back, she said, "Did ya need something, Steve?"

Before he spoke and stuck his foot in his mouth, Steve took a long drink of cool water. How should he word it? He knew whatever he said wouldn't come out right, but there was no help but to ask. "Why ya be so pissed at me?"

Daisy Mae did turn then and swept him from head to foot and back. He'd say he felt like a piece of meat, but he didn't know what to think since she didn't show emotion.

She turned back to the ship's wheel without a word.

So, he had asked wrong. It sounded right to him. He cleared his throat and tried again, more formally, "What have I done to make ya so mad at me?"

There, that sounded right. At least it had her turning back to him.

Steve could have killed JP because just as Daisy Mae opened her mouth to answer, JP yelled, "Land ho."

Chapter Eight

DAISY MAE SPUN around and couldn't believe her eyes. Not only had she been saved from spouting off her mouth, but she'd been shocked at the tiny island. How had she never seen it? Mais, *I've never taken dis route. Why would I? There no be good fishing here.*

JP and Pierre high-fived each other. "*Oui!*" they yelled in unison.

Steve only said, "No fucking way."

As Daisy Mae maneuvered the boat through unfamiliar waters, she carefully spun the wheel and slowed the speed. With the help of her depth finder, she located a route that brought them close to the island yet still at a distance. It was clear that the twins would need to swim part of the way to reach the shore.

"This be as close as I can git." Daisy Mae turned to Steve, her supposed deckhand on the trip. "Drop anchor."

He did that mock salute thing again and rushed off. She wanted to choke him. No, she really wanted to eat up that fine body she'd just perused. It'd been not easy keeping the heat from her expression. But she guessed she'd done that because his expression hadn't changed.

The twins ripped off their shirts and slipped out of their deck shoes. Without another word, they dove into the water, one after the other. Steve, on the other hand, came back to her.

"Will ya be all right alone?" he asked.

You've got to be kidding me! "*Mais oui.*"

"Are ya sure? I can stay here."

"Believe it or not, Steve, I be a big girl now."

"*Oui,*" he said as he walked away, stripping off his shirt and exposing a finely toned body covered in tattoos. "I be noticing." After kicking off his shoes, he followed the twins into what she expected was frigid water.

What da hell was dat supposed to mean? Daisy Mae sighed. What was she going to do with that man? He was going to leave again. She knew it. Even if he asked her to go with him, she wouldn't. She scoffed at the idea of him asking her to go with him. She'd tried that once already. It hadn't worked then, and she doubted it'd work now.

She attempted to keep her mind off the man of her dreams and went below to get a drink. While windy above, the deck below was hotter than Hades. She grabbed water and a donut, then climbed the stairs, shoveling the chocolate-covered goodness into her mouth.

With the satisfaction chocolate gave her, Daisy Mae looked around her. She loved the water. Leaving it was not an option for her. *Don't git ya hopes up, Daisy Mae, just because he say* un *thing dat made ya insides flutter.*

Noticing something in the distance, Daisy Mae grabbed the binoculars and set her food and drink down. The boys had been right about one thing. The boat appeared to be following them. This island was off the beaten path, so who would be fishing or touring here?

Merde. It was probably another treasure hunter. She was sure her brothers hadn't kept their mouths shut about the map. They'd probably talked about it at the bar with people around. Daisy Mae didn't want trouble when she knew the map was fake. All the maps today were except the ones where treasures had already been located.

Sure, Jean Lafitte had supposed hidden treasure around them, but she thought it'd all been found. There had been a significant find at the mansion on another island. That was supposedly Lafitte's.

When the other boat stopped, dropped anchor, and threw out the dive flags, Daisy Mae sighed in relief. The twins were making her paranoid. Someone was diving, and they were still a reasonable distance from them— nothing to worry about.

After checking out the boat and her gauges, Daisy Mae did what she usually did with paying passengers. She pulled out a book. Sure, she helped her passengers set up and bring in their catch, but sometimes, fish didn't bite so greedily. So, she had her backup plan.

It'd been a while since she'd started this particular book. Remembering the plot made her laugh out loud. It was about a treasure hunter who'd returned in time and met the pirate who'd hidden the treasure she'd been seeking. At least that wouldn't happen to her.

Escaping into a world of intrigue and romance, she lost focus on the world around her.

*****

Romeo followed the twins to the island. JP brought out the waterproof bag that held their elusive map. He and

Pierre held it, whispering and pointing. Were they expecting him to hit them over the head and steal the treasure for himself?

Pierre turned around and waved Romeo forward as JP rolled the map and returned it to the pouch. "We gots a hike a'fore us."

Romeo followed the twins, figuring that to be the case, but knowing it couldn't be long since this island appeared small. The island, while it had a rather large sandy beach, also had lush vegetation without trails. So, the twins had found an island no one had explored or at least visited recently. Good on them.

Romeo wondered what Daisy Mae was doing. The hairs on his neck still prickled, and he almost turned around and went to her. Then, he told himself she'd blow the horn if something were wrong.

Pierre asked, "*Chèr*, how long ya stay dis time?"

He followed Pierre, feeling the weight of the situation. He had no clue how things would unfold. He was sure that Daisy Mae's safety was paramount, but he couldn't divulge that to Pierre. "No idea," he muttered, trying to mask his concern. Perhaps today would mark the end of this relentless treasure hunt. Maybe the twins would finally understand that they had been led on a futile pursuit and would abandon it altogether.

As they ducked under overhanging branches, stepped over decaying vegetation, and cautiously avoided numerous snakes, Romeo's thoughts drifted back to each mission he had undertaken while working for HIS in various jungle and wooded environments.

As Bravo's team moved through the dense undergrowth, he and the team leader navigated their way while the others focused on clearing the area. He vividly remembered the times he had to skillfully wield a machete, and there was one close call when he nearly cut his leg. In the aftermath of that incident, his team leader, Grits, entrusted him with the compass, recognizing his lack of expertise in wielding a large knife.

Lost in thought, the first blast of the horn almost passed his notice. The second, however, jolted him into action.

Romeo reacted without hesitation at the sign of trouble. He rushed back through the way they had come, shoving aside tree limbs and leaping over fallen logs in his path. Daisy Mae was in distress, and he was determined to reach her as quickly as possible.

He had spent considerable time navigating the rugged island trail they had tried to maneuver through. Finally, as he emerged onto the beach, the piercing sound of gunfire filled the air. His heart nearly came to a halt as he witnessed a boat zooming past *Seas the Day*, unleashing a storm of gunfire at Daisy Mae and the boat.

Romeo was submerged in the water, his mind disregarding his safety. With an unexpected burst of speed, he propelled himself through the water, reaching the boat in what felt like an astonishingly short time. Unfortunately, the boat firing on Daisy Mae had passed them by, but it appeared to be approaching for a second turn.

Romeo boarded and raced to Daisy Mae, about to pull her into his arms. In an instant, he halted as he watched and listened to her.

"*Mon Dieu!*" she said, checking a Kimber 9mm magazine. "No one shoots at me *bateau*."

When the other boat headed back their way, Romeo reacted. He snatched the gun from Daisy Mae's hand and pushed her behind him. Ducking, he emptied the magazine at the passing boat. When they didn't return for another pass, he sighed with relief.

Romeo turned and embraced Daisy Mae. He regretted following the twins to the island. *Always listen to your gut,* he'd been advised. And he'd ignored it.

It only took a moment to realize how good Daisy Mae felt in his arms. She fit perfectly with her head on his shoulder, just below his chin.

She relaxed into him, then, as if catching herself, she stiffened and pushed away. "If ya ever do that again, *couyon*, I'll shoot ya meself."

"Ya be welcome," he said. Romeo didn't know what just happened. He'd protected her. Wasn't that what all women wanted?

"Never, grab me weapon again."

Okay. So that was it. Maybe he shouldn't have grabbed it without asking. But there had been no time. "Next time, I won't."

She pushed on his chest. "There best not be a next time."

He continued to step back while she walked forward, constantly pushing at his chest. He grinned. Boy, she was sexy when she was feisty.

Romeo stopped and grabbed her hands when his legs hit the boat railing. "It's okay to admit ya was scared. I won't tell anyone."

"Get off me *bateau*!" she demanded.

Chapter Nine

"*MERDE*. OF ALL the egotistical things ta do!" Daisy Mae still fumed on the boat ride back to Bayou Junction. She'd allowed Steve to remain on the boat, but only at her brother's pleading. Okay, so she wouldn't have left him stranded on the island, but the desire had flittered through her to do so.

Daisy Mae hated treasure hunting. Look what had happened. Her boat had been riddled with bullets, leaving holes in numerous places. Fortunately, the damage appeared to be above the waterline, but the repairs would be time-consuming. She had to fix them before taking out another charter, as no passenger would feel safe seeing the damage.

She wondered who had shot at her. It had to be another treasure hunter, but which one? Where had her big-mouthed brothers spouted off about their map? There are too many places to know them.

"*Deyzee Mè*," Pierre asked. "What did da other *bateau* look like?"

Like he cared. The twins wanted to return to the island and continue searching for the treasure, but she overrode their desire. She would not sit there and wait for the other boat to return.

"Why do it matter?" she asked, turning the wheel and slowing the engine, bringing them into the channel surrounding the docks.

Pierre shrugged. "Jus' curious."

With narrowed eyes, Daisy Mae swore. He had an idea who it was. "*Mon Dieu!* Spill."

Suddenly, Pierre looked all innocent. "What do ya mean?"

"Who shot at me *bateau*?"

Pierre shook his head. "No idea."

She didn't believe him but let it go for now. She knew JP was the weaker of her brothers, so she'd get him alone another time and find out the truth about everything —including where they acquired the map.

Could it be the stolen map, and the owner wanted it back in any way he could, including violence? She had to know before she put herself in danger again. She wouldn't even put her asshole brothers in danger if she could help it.

"Thanks for allowing me to go with ya today."

When had Steve learned to sneak up on people so stealthily? That was an eerie habit. "Thank *mon frères*," she snapped.

Daisy Mae knew she needed to calm herself. She was becoming a downright bitch, but hell, she'd been shot at today. Steve only did what solid and alpha men did. He took control of the situation.

Only Steve hadn't been a strong, alpha male when she'd known him before. He'd been polite and never made fun of her when her brothers did. Steve would take up for her and include her in their activities most of the time. Or, he'd spend extra time with her when her brothers wouldn't.

As soon as she understood that feeling, she was fascinated with him. As a young girl, she fantasized about marrying him. As Daisy Mae had grown into a teenager, she'd continued that fantasy. He'd left without a backward glance when she'd tried to turn it into reality. Her dream had burned to ashes.

"I be sorry," Steve said softly.

Knowing she should accept his apology, she sighed. "*Bien*." Then she spun on him. "Just don't do it again." Circling back to guide the boat to the dock, Daisy Mae realized she'd left a chance for him to do it again.

Next thing she knew, Steve stood on the dock, tying off the boat. How had he moved so fast? What did they teach at the FBI academy that honed his skills and confidence? It only made him sexier than before. *Merde.* She had to get him out of her mind.

The twins grabbed their gear and exited the boat. "*Au revoir, Deyzee Mè*," they said in unison.

Daisy Mae almost exploded at them. Au revoir, Deyzee Mè? *Not, I be sorry I got ya* bateau *shot up, and ya nearly killed,* Deyzee Mè?

Steve jumped back on the boat. Grabbing his gear, he turned to her. "I be willing to help ya repair the *bateau*."

If she didn't have a charter in the morning, she'd tell him where to put his offer of help, but as it was, she needed the assistance. She needed help patching the holes enough to make them look presentable tomorrow. The boat would require professional repair, but they could make it work now.

Daisy Mae sighed in relent. "*Merci.*"

Growing up where Steve had, Daisy Mae hadn't needed to show him what to do. Only, they'd shared the same materials, sometimes touching hands. Each time that happened, a spark shot through her.

She still wanted him, and it irked her beyond all reason.

"I be sorry da twins no help ya."

Daisy Mae wasn't sure when, in her lifetime, everyone had stopped referring to her brothers as JP and Pierre but as "*da* twins." Maybe because they had been the only twins in their tiny town while growing up.

"*Mais,*"—she pushed the bill of her cap up—"it be expected."

Steve stopped sanding a spot he'd just filled. "So, dey treat ya da same as before?"

Before what? Before you abandoned us? Me? She shrugged. "Dey be who dey be."

"Why haven't ya left this town and settled in a bigger fishing community?" Steve asked. "Ya could build a fleet of charters somewhere else and make a mint."

Her heart said, "Because I've waited for ya to come home," while her tongue lashed out, "*Mais,* ya leaving don't mean everyone wants to leave."

"*Touché!*" Steve touched his chest in mock pain. "I always thought ya wanted ta leave."

I had. With you. "Schoolgirl fancy. I no need a bigger town to rebuild the fleet."

"True." Steve set down his supplies. "Done. Want to inspect my work?"

Mais, oui. She needed to ensure it would suffice for tomorrow. While they'd learned to care for a boat growing up, they'd never had to fill bullet holes.

Daisy Mae strode over to him. Steve didn't move back. She felt…crowded…hot…wanting. *Merde!*

"It be fine," she finally choked out after being so near him and his shirtless self. She'd been avoiding looking at him for that reason. His artfully designed chest drew her anyhow. Childhood fantasies….

Steve smiled. "*Bien*. How 'bout a drink ta cool down?"

"*Non*" would have been her first response, but she wanted to be near him. This confused her. She wanted him but didn't want to like him because he'd broken her heart once, and she didn't want it to happen again. Good grief. She sounded like a girl still in love with the boy who always rescued her from her brothers—or a girl in a romance novel. *Mon Dieu! Not that*.

"*Non, merci*," she said, knowing it was the correct answer—not the answer she wanted, but the right one.

"Come on. Are ya chicken ta be wit me?"

That set off her ire. "*Oui*, I have a drink wit ya," she ultimately said. Why not? Maybe she would learn enough about him to douse the flames licking inside her for him. Just maybe….

His resulting grin shot that idea all to hell. She was in trouble.

Chapter Ten

ROMEO AND DAISY Mae were seated at Duke's, a cozy bar illuminated by a stained-glass dangling light. The savory aroma of fried fish and the rich scent of a freshly poured pitcher of draft beer filled the air. Despite the inviting atmosphere, an uncomfortable silence enveloped them as they contemplated their menu choices. Daisy Mae took the lead and spoke with the waitress, as Romeo, living up to his nickname, found himself at a loss for words in the presence of the beautiful server.

Compared to other women, Romeo found it effortless to engage in conversation with Daisy Mae. He assumed this was mainly because of the bond they had developed while growing up together. Understanding the significance of their longstanding relationship, Romeo chose not to dissect or jeopardize something already working well.

Upon gulping beer, Daisy Mae suddenly exclaimed, "Why did ya leave m—" She quickly covered her mouth as she coughed. He suspected the cough was feigned but decided to keep quiet. "*Merde*, why did ya leave so fast?"

The woman confronted him with unyielding directness. Unable to disclose the truth, he clung to the familiar tale he had recounted for years: "I had an opportunity to attend college and seized it." As he sipped his beer and gingerly rested it on the coaster bearing the Duke's logo, placed there by the attentive server, he added, "Plus, there wasn't much tethering me to dis place."

Daisy Mae sputtered and coughed as the beer caught in her throat, causing Romeo to quickly shift his attention to ensure she was okay. After a few moments, she waved her hand for him to continue.

So, he continued with some truth. "*Mamau* and Papa wanted me to have adventures, travel, and experience things I couldn't find in dis small town. So, dey encouraged me to go."

He couldn't speak of that night with her. How would things have been different if he'd taken her with him? No, she'd been too young to know her mind.

She gazed at him intently for a moment, her scrutinizing gaze making him feel uncomfortable in the confined space of the booth. "Why didn't ya bother coming back to visit?"

As he sipped his beer, he suddenly felt a strong urge to spit it out. He struggled to find the right words to explain that his feelings for her had changed from friendship to something more romantic. However, he couldn't deny that she had always been off-limits, as she was his best friend's sister. Instead, he shrugged. "Dere be no time. I stayed busy with college, my job with the FBI, and my current job with HIS. I video-chatted with *Mamau* and Papa, so we visited plenty."

Daisy Mae gently shook her head, her expression filled with compassion. "That wasn't the same; ya *maman* and papa truly missed ya."

Romeo felt the sharp impact in the pit of his stomach, causing him to look down instinctively. His eyes focused on the surface of his beer glass as he absentmindedly traced his finger along the smooth rim, lost in thought. Romeo had anticipated their response, but they had reassured him to embrace life and not dwell on their absence from it. Above all, he yearned for the warmth of his mother's embrace and his father's encouraging pats on the back. However, as time passed, he realized he couldn't alter the past.

Exhausted from the emotional turmoil of being drawn to a woman unlike any other, he boldly decided to change the dynamics of their relationship. "Why didn't ya leave Bayou Junction?" He wanted to spout out "I know how badly you wanted to leave." But, instead said, "Why stay? I heard ya had an academic scholarship offer. Why ya no take it?" He popped a nacho chip piled with chicken, cheese, lettuce, tomato, sour cream, jalapeno, and guacamole into his mouth to halt his urge to ask more. He had numerous questions for her but knew he had to approach them slowly. *Like—Is it true what ya brother said about ya liking me? I'd thought it a ploy to leave town, not that ya really wanted me.*

Daisy Mae delicately grasped her glass, giving it a gentle swirl as she fixed her gaze upon the rich amber liquid in the beer mug. "How did ya hear about dat?" She looked up at him and raised a brow.

Romeo put on his "duh" face. "Remember, ya brothers, and I be friends. We chatted *beaucoup* when I first left." He stopped. When he discovered a chance

Daisy Mae might come to his college, he decided to sever all ties with her brothers to find solace and distance himself from her.

"*Mais, oui.*" Just as their dinners were brought, she finished the last bite of the crispy nacho plate. Both had chosen the day's catch from Bayou Junction's waters, served with a colorful assortment of fresh, steamed vegetables and golden, buttery potatoes. Despite Romeo's indifference towards the veggies, they were a part of the meal plate. He'd push them aside, focusing on the succulent fish and the comforting presence of potatoes prepared in some delicious form.

When Daisy Mae closed her mouth around a bite of fish, closed her eyes, and moaned, Romeo's dick reacted. Like an inexperienced youth, he couldn't restrain it around Daisy Mae. It seemed to have a mind of its own. Lord, he was in trouble.

Not sure what to ask next, Romeo quickly looked away and shoveled some mashed potatoes into his mouth. He still needed to remember his previous question.

Realizing she wouldn't answer, he swallowed and tried a different conversation. "How be business?"

Daisy Mae gently pressed her lips together to one side, her brow furrowing in concern before she spoke. "It feels like everything, it be moving slower with each day. Bayou Junction be like a hidden gem compared to de other destinations near here. We no actively promote our town to tourists, but somehow dey always manage to find dere way here. Or, at least, dey used to."

He could no longer withhold the burning question on his mind: "Are ya planning to venture out *encore* after someone took a shot at ya?" After contacting the sheriff's office, Alice arranged to meet them at Duke's to gather their statement and assess the repaired damage. Fortunately, Daisy Mae had taken photos of the damage before it was repaired.

"*Mais oui*."

He stilled his fork. "Are ya kidding me? Someone shot at ya. You don't know who or why. It could happen again."

Daisy Mae sighed loudly. "Steve, leave it be. I be a big girl and can take care of meself."

Romeo decided she was mad. "Well, then, I'm going with ya."

Her fork clattered as she dropped it to the plate, and the sound ricocheted in the room. "*Mais non!*"

"Why not? What's the problem?"

"'Cause I no need ya. You be in de way."

"No, I won't, and I be going."

Daisy Mae closed her beautiful eyes. "*Merde*." She opened them again and pinned his stare. "Ya work. Me hands be due for vacation."

He believed it to be a triumph despite his belief that she would keep him occupied enough to avoid any chance of their paths crossing. Little did she know about his true capabilities.

Romeo engaged in light conversation as they finished their meal, touching on various small topics such as the current weather, local events, updates about their families, and anything else he considered to be non-controversial.

Daisy Mae carefully set down her silverware on the table, taking a moment to draw in a deep breath. "Steve, why dis chit-chat?" she asked, looking at him intently. "That no be you. What it be ya want to know?"

She had managed to capture him unawares. He had underestimated how well she knew him before he departed from town. "I want ta know da real reason ya stay."

Daisy Mae raised her brows in a challenge. "*Mais*, I want ta know da *real* reason ya left."

Absorbed in the moment, Romeo became acutely aware of the impasse they had reached. As he delicately placed his silverware on the table and briskly wiped his mouth with the napkin, his eyes remained fixated on Daisy Mae, observing her every subtle movement and expression. Her gaze fixed on him with an enigmatic expression he struggled to interpret. It wasn't one of joy or sorrow; it simply was. Her eyes gleamed brightly, drawing him in as he yearned for her to reciprocate his feelings. At that thought, Romeo's dick jerked and hardened.

"Truth?" he asked.

She nodded. "Truth."

The moment had arrived to reveal the truth. He realized they could carve out some time to be together while he was visiting. Then, he wouldn't have to jerk off thinking of her.

Well, here goes nothing. "You."

Chapter Eleven

DAISY MAE FELT like she might have choked on her beer if she had taken a sip when Steve uttered his unexpected words. She had harbored the hope that he had deep feelings for her and couldn't bear to be apart from her. However, she had long moved on from that schoolgirl fantasy. Over time, she had become more grounded in reality, fully aware that their relationship could never evolve beyond friendship.

Pointing a thumb at her chest, she asked, "*Moi*?"

Before Steve could respond, Alice eagerly waved and called out to them. "*Bonjour*, Daisy Mae," she greeted as she smoothly slid into the booth next to Daisy Mae. "*Bonjour*, Steve."

Looking green around the gills, Steve nodded. "*Bonjour*."

Mais non! Daisy Mae silently requested that Alice leave the room. She and Steve needed to conclude their conversation, and Daisy Mae was eager to understand why Steve had accused her of keeping him away when she'd offered to go with him. Was that why he stayed away? Because he thought she'd try again to convince him to take her with him.

Little did he know, she'd grown from that little girl who'd thrown herself at her first crush to keep from losing him.

Marie—their waitress, appeared with a beer for her sister and then disappeared without a word.

Daisy Mae picked up her beverage. "Drinking on duty?" she asked Alice.

Alice took a long drag on the beer. "Shift be jus' done."

"I thought ya was here ta take our statements." Daisy Mae said.

Nodding, Alice turned to Daisy Mae. "I be. I decided ta do it off duty ta have a drink together. It's been forever since Steve be in town."

Daisy Mae felt a surge of burning jealousy coursing through her veins. Although Steve was not her beau, she did not want him to be only a friend. Given his nickname, "Romeo," she suspected that he had the power to seduce any woman he desired.

In a fit of childishness, she wanted to cross her arms over her chest and pout to get Steve's attention. Instead, she kept Alice's focus on her by retelling the day's events.

Alice made notes in a small notebook. When Daisy Mae finished, Alice asked, "Steve, da ya have anyting ta add?"

Steve shifted. "*Non.*"

Alice put the notebook in her uniform breast pocket and shook her head. "I no believe we've got some rogue shooter out dere. We no can have dat in our waters."

"*Mais*," Daisy Mae said, "I not sure it were a rogue."

Tilting her head in interest, Alice asked, "How so?"

Daisy Mae met Steve's eyes as he shook his head in disapproval. Disregarding her brothers' insistence on secrecy, she had already confessed to Alice about the map. "We were treasure hunting," she explained, refusing to let anyone deter her from the truth.

Alice clamped her lips tight before speaking. "Is dat de map ya told us 'bout?"

Without looking at Steve and receiving his disapproval, Daisy Mae nodded.

"I sure would like to git me hands on it and see if it be da stolen one."

Daisy Mae took that like a slap in the face. Her spine went ramrod straight. "Are ya saying me *frères* are thieves? Dey be many things, but thieves dey no be."

Alice put up a hand that halted Daisy Mae's words. "Hoo boy, I no say dat."

Daisy Mae harumphed. That's precisely what her friend had said.

Why didn't Steve defend her brothers? He looked as though he would rather be anywhere but there. At that moment, Daisy Mae realized that he had misspoken when he said he only stayed away because of her. That wasn't what he'd meant at all.

Ready to finish her conversation with Steve, Daisy Mae asked to be let out of the booth, surprising Alice and Steve as she realized they'd never get a private moment together at the bar. "Steve, ya ready ta git back to da *bateau*?"

He quickly straightened up and nodded, mirroring Alice's movement as she rose from her seat. Steve had barely exchanged three words with Alice. She couldn't help but feel that her friend was somewhat undeserving of the tinge of jealousy that she felt.

"Be careful, Daisy Mae. Would ya like me ta go out wit ya? I doubt anyone would mess wit ya if ya had a deputy sheriff aboard."

Daisy Mae carefully considered the option before ultimately dismissing it. After all, Steve had already stepped up, and she had ungratefully accepted his offer.

She hugged Alice. "It jus' be a simple fishing charter, *mais* we see how things go."

After their farewell, Daisy Mae waved to Marie as she approached the exit. Steve shook Alice's hand, expressing his appreciation. *Wow. He'd spoken.*

She pondered how he came to be known as Romeo if he couldn't even speak around women. She mentally shook her head and observed that he was polite, allowing Daisy Mae to take the lead. Furthermore, she recalled that he had never shown any interest in Alice during their time in school.

As Steve and she walked to the door, she felt his hand lightly touch her back. A jolt of electricity ran through her. His touch, even so gentle, was enough to send her libido into overdrive.

Merde. She wanted him. Even though she didn't want to, she did. And she wanted him in every way possible.

Once they exited Duke's, his hand dropped, and he walked beside her to the docks. "Was dere something ya needed us ta do on the *bateau*?"

The audacity! Was he seriously joking with her? After accusing her of being his reason for not returning, he actually believed she wanted to fix her boat. Men really had no idea.

"*Non.*" Her tone may have been more terse than she'd meant.

"What den?"

Daisy Mae felt her face turn bright red as steam billowed from her ears. She abruptly stopped and whipped around to face Steve. "*Mon Dieu*! Do ya be kidding me?" she exclaimed, eyes narrowed in disbelief.

Looking confused and a bit uncomfortable, Steve looked at her. "'Bout what?"

She wanted to pace. She wanted to rant. Yet, she stood her ground. "After da bomb ya dropped in dere, ya think me no want to finish dat conversation?"

As he scuffed his feet along the weathered wooden planks of the dock, Steve's unease manifested in the hesitant rhythm of the movement. When he finally mustered the courage to raise his eyes, the anguish in his gaze shattered her heart into a thousand pieces. "*Mais*, I didn't mean it," he uttered, his voice cracking with remorse.

She was going to kill the man. And she had the boat to dump him so his friends would never know. "*Oui*, ya did mean it, *mais* ya didn't explain how ya meant it."

"Let's sit on da *bateau, et* we talk."

The plan worked well for her. They proceeded along the brief dock and then boarded her vessel. She gracefully made her way over to the two captain's chairs positioned at the front of the boat, knowing that these seats were where her clients would settle in to enjoy a day of fishing. She knew they could swivel, allowing her to effortlessly turn around and get a good look at the person she was speaking to.

Steve cleared his throat as they settled into their seats to indicate he was about to speak. "I meant that ya were why I didn't return."

Her heart was pounding loudly in her chest, the sound echoing in her ears. She needed to understand the reason behind it. "Why, exactly?" she asked, her voice filled with urgency and determination. Had she kept him away with her antics the night before he left?

Steve closed his eyes momentarily, then bored his gaze into hers. "'Cause I wanted ya, *et* ya be my best friend's *souer*. I couldn't have ya and didn't think I could stop meself from going after ya."

Daisy Mae was surprised at the turn of events, but she thoroughly enjoyed it. The thought of being with Steve made her stomach somersault with excitement. Despite her previous declaration that they couldn't be a couple due to their geographical separation—he in Baltimore and she in Bayou Junction—the temptation of spending just one night with him was irresistible. The thought of it was utterly invigorating and tantalizing.

With her words tumbling out before her mind could catch up, she exclaimed, "That be da most stupid thing I ever did hear."

Chapter Twelve

SURPRISED BY THE remark, Romeo started to say something but stopped himself. He felt his anger welling up inside at being labeled as stupid. He knew that she hadn't explicitly called him stupid but referred to the bro code as such. The bro code was a revered and solemn agreement among men.

"It no be stupid," he nearly bellowed, his frustration evident in his tone. "It be our code."

Daisy Mae rolled her eyes. "Let me guess—guy code or something equally as stupid?"

Now, he felt tiny. "Bro code," he mumbled.

"Like I said—stupid."

He pondered the situation. Despite feeling at ease in Daisy Mae's presence, he was far from being a smooth-talking Romeo. He found himself at a loss for actions when it came to her.

"Before ya say something else equally as stupid, let me sum it up. Ya no come home 'cause of ya feelings for me, and me brother happened ta be ya best friend."

With a sense of caution about the direction things were heading, Romeo nodded in acknowledgment.

"Did ya ever once think of how I might feel?"

Merde. He'd thought of nothing but the night before he'd left, but he'd felt she didn't mean it or know what she'd been offering. But, had Pierre been correct? Despite her anger, had he actually detected a hint of sexual tension from her? His radar seemed off, making him wonder if he had imagined it.

Overwhelmed with diminutiveness, Romeo hunched his shoulders like a young boy caught with his hand in the cookie jar and let out a quiet, barely audible murmur. "*Non.*" This was out of character, but he acknowledged his mistake and struggled to accept it.

"*Merde.*"

Romeo felt the warmth of Daisy Mae's presence as she drew near, and he lifted his gaze to meet her eyes—brilliant, sparkling orbs filled with excitement. "And," Romeo cleared his throat, "what would ya have said?" *Let her say* oui. He didn't fully grasp what was transpiring with Daisy Mae, but he longed for her to desire him as much as he desired her.

"Let me show ya," she whispered as she gently raised her hand, pulled his head towards her, and closed her eyes as she pressed her lips against his.

Merde. His heart raced with excitement as he fervently wrapped her in his arms, pulling her close as he deepened the kiss. Finally holding Daisy Mae in his arms, he felt a sense of completeness, as if everything was falling into place just as he had anticipated. That corny line of "You complete me" buzzed through his mind, and he knew it was true.

In an instant, as if time had stopped, he found his cock hardened by her presence. Feeling an overwhelming need to express his deep yearning for Daisy Mae, Romeo savored the sensation of their bodies uniting in perfect harmony.

As their tongues danced, she moaned into his mouth. The blood in his body rushed south, leaving him lightheaded with desire. Romeo was at a crossroads, knowing he needed to halt his actions or risk taking her immediately. The uncertainty of her desires lingered in the air. She had shown enough interest in kissing him, but what more did she want?

Navigating relationships with women always left him feeling perplexed. He was never in a long-term relationship because of his fear of making the wrong move and his tendency to rush through the bases to ensure the woman was pleased. He pondered the possibility of savoring every moment with Daisy Mae, truly understanding her preferences at each stage of their relationship.

Leaning his forehead against hers, he rasped, "So, ya really meant it that night?"

Daisy Mae pushed on his chest to put room between them. She narrowed her eyes at Romeo. "Ya fool. I offered meself to ya. How could ya not tell?"

All he could manage to utter was a simple "Oh."

Daisy Mae gently withdrew from his embrace, creating distance as she instinctively folded her arms in a protective stance across her chest. "Ya took Shelly to prom when I had hinted and hinted, even buying a dress 'cause I was sure ya'd invite me."

What an ass he had been to her. Romeo had taken Shelly to the prom because he knew Daisy Mae's brothers would not have allowed him to go with her. However, he also knew that by taking Shelly, there was a good chance that Daisy Mae would be present at the prom since the two women were best friends. In his teenage mind, this seemed like a logical solution to his predicament. He realized it was not the most rational decision, but at seventeen, he was willing to try anything to navigate the complexities of teenage social dynamics.

Romeo reached out with a gentle but firm grip, drawing her back into the warmth of his embrace. As he held her tightly, their two bodies melted into one, finding solace in each other's presence. "I be sorry, Daisy Mae." Not that he still could have done anything about Daisy Mae's feelings back then—except to break her heart.

At this moment, he finally felt a sense of relief, knowing that he no longer had to fret about Daisy Mae's brothers. With no best friend among them, Daisy Mae now had the freedom to make her own choices as she was old enough to do so.

Merde. Romeo spent years pining for Daisy Mae, wishing he hadn't wasted so much time when they could have been together. But, as much as he wanted her in bed right now, he needed to show her how he felt about her, not just sexually.

As Daisy Mae's arms unfolded and enveloped his back, Romeo sensed the dampness of her tears seeping through his shirt. Despite her silence, her embrace conveyed the depth of her sorrow.

"Oh, *chère*," he whispered as he settled his head on her. "I be sorry."

"Ya be a big fool," she said through sniffles.

He knew, deep down, that he had acted foolishly before. After tenderly kissing her forehead, he quietly admitted, "*Oui*, I be."

Her voice was soft as she lay against his chest, asking, "Are ya going ta ask me on a date or what?"

Romeo's lips curled into a smile as he mulled it over. He admired Daisy Mae's directness and cherished that quality in her. "I be considering it," he admitted with a grin.

Daisy Mae tilted her head back and squinted, her eyes narrowing as she spoke sharply, "Think faster."

Chuckling, Romeo rubbed his hands up and down her small back. "*Chère*, would ya like to go on a date with me?"

She nodded. "*Mais oui*." Then she stood on tiptoes and kissed him again. This time, her mouth left his before he could respond, but that didn't diminish the heat that flowed through their brief connection.

"Why did ya stop?"

"I'll save da rest for me date." Daisy Mae pushed herself away from the embrace of Romeo's arms. "I've had a trying day. I'm going ta call it quits."

Was he being dismissed? It certainly seemed like it. The situation was almost comical, making him want to laugh again. Daisy Mae always tried to dominate her brothers while growing up. Then, Romeo's mind raced to sex again. Was she a kinky sort?

He was transfixed and unable to move, captivated by his thoughts. He'd always been a plain vanilla kind of guy. He had experimented with many positions but had never explored anything wild or kinky. Okay, maybe a bit kinky, but only a bit.

Knowing that the answer to his next question would most likely be negative, he asked anyway. His mother had ingrained in him the habit of always acting like a gentleman. "May I escort ya to ya truck?" he inquired.

Daisy Mae thought for a moment and then sighed. "*Oui*."

Surprisingly, he was taken aback by her response. Given her earlier dismissal of him, he had anticipated a refusal. "*Bien*, let's go," he said.

They disembarked from the boat and strolled along the pier to the parking lot. Romeo desired a physical connection with her, so he kept his hand on her back as they walked. As he caught sight of her opening her truck door, he endeavored to lean in and kiss her goodnight.

Daisy Mae put up a hand to his lips. "Date."

Once more taken aback, he leaned back and looked at her closely. Was she fucking with him? The intensity in her gaze indicated that she wasn't playing around. Was she being coy? It didn't seem like his Daisy Mae.

"Date," he agreed. "Tomorrow *soir*?" He had decided not to wait any longer for her presence or involvement.

Before she sat in her truck, she nodded. "*Demain soir*."

Romeo closed the door and watched her drive away. Tonight had been a whirlwind of confusion for him. He needed to sit down and carefully contemplate everything that had transpired to make sense of it all.

After learning that she genuinely harbored feelings for him, he was determined to persist until she comprehended that she belonged to him.

Chapter Thirteen

ROMEO PEERED OVER his steaming cup of coffee at his mother. "Are ya sure it be okay if I don't go to da hospital 'til later?" Guilt plagued him for leaving his *maman* for Daisy Mae. He had to remember it was at his papa's request.

Barbara shook her head. "Go, Steve. I know ya papa be worried 'bout Daisy Mae, et now dat someone shot at her, we both expect ya be dere protecting her. *Mais*, dey might release him today."

With a glimmer of hope in his eyes, Steve nodded and forced a smile, desperately wishing that things would turn out in their favor. He cherished and longed for his parents, just as he yearned for the home where he spent his formative years until he left for college. After taking another sip of the hot brew, he stood up. It was time to go.

Today, Romeo was visibly armed. He grabbed his backpack and kissed his mother on the cheek. "Lock up after I leave," he instructed.

She stood and followed him to the door.

"Keep me updated on Papa, if you please."

Tears shimmered in his mother's eyes as she spoke, "You no worry 'bout us. Take care of dat *petite fille*."

Romeo nodded, unsure how his *maman* considered Daisy Mae a "little girl," but he guessed that was her Southern coming out in her.

At the wheel of his dad's sturdy truck, Romeo made his way to the quiet docks and skillfully maneuvered into a parking spot. As the first light of dawn broke over the water, the red glints of alligator eyes became visible in his headlights, casting an eerie glow over the landscape. It was just another typical day in Louisiana.

Romeo looked around the parking lot and spotted Daisy Mae's truck. He wondered how she would respond to his presence that day, thinking back to her fearless demeanor the previous night. A smile spread across his face. Indeed, Romeo had selected a remarkable partner for life.

Contemplating a lifetime together, he nodded to himself. He realized that he would need to find a way to persuade her to spend the rest of her life with him. Whether they relocated to Baltimore or stayed in Bayou Junction, he didn't care as long as she was his.

Checking the status of his weapon and ensuring it was ready for any potential trouble, Romeo holstered it at his side. After grabbing his backpack, he exited the truck, locked it, and pocketed the key fob.

As he strolled down the brief dock, he couldn't help but notice the hustle and bustle of people on their boats, some embarking on charters while others enjoyed the privacy of their vessels. Stopping at *Seas the Day*, he worried when he didn't spy Daisy Mae on deck.

When Romeo heard loud cursing rising from below, he smiled. "Permission to board," he yelled. Romeo vowed never to attempt sneaking up on Daisy Mae again. He had learned the hard way that she didn't appreciate his particular talent.

The sun had risen above the horizon, and Romeo knew it would be another sweltering day. When Daisy Mae emerged from below, the light caught her face, revealing adorable but grease-stained features.

With a dirty rag in her hand, she waved him aboard. "*Bonjour!* Do ya know anything 'bout *bateau* engines?"

Romeo didn't have a clue about the boat engine, but he would still attempt to help Daisy Mae. As he stepped onto the boat, the weight of his backpack hit the bench with a thud. He made his way across the deck toward her.

Daisy Mae narrowed her eyes at his waist, then looked up at him. "Dat be necessary?"

Romeo nodded in acknowledgment, the weight of her words sinking in as he realized she was referring to his firearm. "*Mais oui.*"

Daisy Mae rolled her eyes. "*Mon Dieu!* We no going anywhere if I can't turn dis engine over."

"I know my way around a truck engine. They can't be much different." Romeo was aware of their differences, yet he endeavored to bring a smile to Daisy Mae's face with a lighthearted comment.

It worked perfectly.

Her smile brightened her entire face. Daisy Mae handed him the wrench in her dirty hand and said, "Go 'head, *couyon.*"

Romeo graciously accepted the wrench, and with a sense of anticipation, he drew closer to Daisy Mae. Gently, he brushed his lips against hers, reveling in the tenderness of her lips. Reluctantly, he eventually brought the kiss to a close with a lingering, affectionate peck. "Good morning, Rocket."

"Why do ya call—"

"*Bonjour*," a voice called from the dock.

Romeo could have sworn that he heard Daisy Mae growl with an unmistakable air of disapproval as they turned around.

"What ya want, Mario?" Daisy Mae asked, not too kindly.

"What be going on?" Mario asked.

"What does it look like is going on, you *couyon*?" Daisy Mae asked.

"Careful, the mosquitoes be big." And the man walked away.

The mosquitoes be big. What did that mean? "Who dat be?"

Daisy Mae grunted. "Mario Xenos. Me rival."

The man's demeanor and words immediately caught Romeo's attention, almost as if he had set off an alarm on Romeo's radar. It became evident that it would be highly advantageous to Mario if Daisy Mae sold out her operation. Romeo needed to learn more about the man, such as Mario's whereabouts yesterday when he and Daisy Mae were under fire on the boat. It wasn't just treasure hunters that would benefit from her absence on the water.

"Come on,"—Daisy Mae waved—"let's get dis engine going. I have a charter in *une heure*."

Romeo didn't know how to help, but he would use all his knowledge of engines to assist Daisy Mae.

Ultimately, Daisy Mae found it necessary to cancel the charter. She cursed a storm when she realized someone had tampered with her boat. Sabotage after a shooting, didn't sit well with Romeo. Something was rotten in Bayou Junction, and it centered around his Daisy Mae.

He realized he needed a capable investigator on the ground so that he could provide round-the-clock protection for Daisy Mae. He was confident he knew the right men to call for the job.

Before doing anything else, he needed to ensure everything was in place for date night while ensuring Daisy Mae remained within his view. Romeo knew she wouldn't react well to his protectiveness, but she would have to deal with it. It was in her best interest and his sanity.

"How 'bout we visit my papa in the hospital since ya have to wait for da part to repair da *bateau*? *Mamau* would love ta see ya." It'd also keep her by his side.

Daisy Mae closed her eyes and let out a heavy sigh. He was keenly aware that her reaction wasn't prompted by his request but rather by the weight of everything that had transpired in her life. Canceling the charter today cost her money. Mario was free when the four men were looking to go fishing. Romeo could feel Daisy Mae's heartbreak when she approached Mario and asked if he could accommodate her passengers. However, putting her clients first, she persevered and made the necessary arrangements.

He was proud of her but suspicious that Mario was conveniently free when her engine was sabotaged. Only he couldn't ponder that at the moment.

Keep her by his side, call the guys, take her on a memorable date, and get to at least second base tonight. Those were his priorities, in order of necessity, not desirability.

Chapter Fourteen

THE HOSPITAL CHOSE to keep Romeo's father one more night for observation. Thankfully, his papa was on the mend.

While Daisy Mae and his mom talked to his papa, he excused himself and stepped out of the room.

It was time to call his team leader. He knew the team was on a much-needed break, but Alpha team was deployed, and Charlie team was still building and training. Romeo selected the correct speed dial on his cell and pushed "Call."

"Grits," his boss answered on the first ring.

"*Bonjour, cher.*"

"What's up, Romeo?"

Romeo anxiously rubbed the back of his neck as he glanced down the brightly lit hall, ensuring Daisy Mae was still lingering in his father's room. He was determined to keep her in the dark about the impending visit from the men coming to investigate on his behalf. She believed that the agents of HIS were on vacation with

Romeo. Although he despised lying to her, he knew she would reject any offer of assistance.

"I have a problem and need help. I know the team be off, *mais* I could use some local investigation."

Romeo could hear fingers snapping, signaling that his team leader had brought someone else into the room. He hoped his leader wasn't in bed with someone, as it would undoubtedly dampen their plans.

"I'm putting you on speaker. Casper is here. Now, tell us what's going on."

Casper, an enigmatic operative with a knack for eerie assignments, formed a solid and effective partnership with Grits. This close bond often sparked jealousy in Romeo, who held the second position in their team. Romeo suspected that the nature of their special operations work led to a faster, deeper connection, but he acknowledged that other pressing matters needed their attention.

"Someone be trying to harm me woman."

"Your woman?" Casper asked, sounding way too bewildered by the statement. "When did this come about?"

"It no matter," Romeo bit out. "I need some help from Bravo."

"What's happened?" Grits asked.

"*Merde,* besides being shot at?"

"What the fuck?" Grits nearly shouted.

"I be fine. We be fine," Romeo bit out again. He needed Grits to stay focused—no time for playing around bullshit.

"Anything else we need to know about?" Grits asked.

"Besides sabotage? I no think so."

"Why do you think this is happening?" Casper asked.

"If I knew, I wouldn't need ya, *couyon*," Romeo snapped.

"Don't get your panties in a bunch. Casper and I will be there tomorrow."

"*Merci, cher.*"

"What about me?" Casper asked.

Romeo ended the call without a word to the agent.

That gave him the opportunity for a date night tonight. There was no way around it. He would have to stay over to protect her. His dick twitched at the thought of what they could do to fill the time.

Romeo reentered the room, his eyes fixated on Daisy Mae. She greeted him with a radiant smile. She was petite, agile, and quick to react like a little pocket rocket. Daisy Mae seemed unchanged in these aspects since his last visit home.

Romeo turned his gaze to his father. "Papa, what can we get ya for breakfast? I tried da cafeteria already. Ya want takeout."

Wayne smiled at that. "Me could use a grilled steak *et* potato. Ya *mère* already say no to dat. How 'bout a breakfast sandwich? Sausage *et* egg."

The family immediately began brainstorming ideas for fast food places that served a good breakfast.

After his papa agreed to a place, Romeo and Daisy Mae left to pick up the food, leaving his parents alone. His mom looked beat. It was fortunate that his father was being released the next day. Romeo wasn't sure if his mom could handle more time with his dad not at home.

Neither Romeo nor Daisy Mae spoke as they exited the room and entered the elevator. Romeo took a chance and reached for Daisy Mae's hand; she didn't jerk away but wrapped her small hand in his.

The profound connection between Romeo and Daisy Mae brought peace to his mind and warmth to his heart. With Daisy Mae standing by his side, he found assurance that everything would turn out just fine. He was determined to protect her body while she, in turn, would be the guardian of his soul. The soul he'd lost during those many interrogations and ops that went sideways.

Sadly, Romeo had to release Daisy Mae's hand to open the truck door for her. After she climbed in, he walked around to the driver's side. Since leaving his papa's room, he'd scanned for potential threats. Someone wanted Daisy Mae's charter business shut down. Did they also want her dead? The thought terrified him. He'd never allow that to happen. He'd bring the entire HIS operation here to protect her if he had to.

"How were me *mère* and *père*?" Romeo asked. He had noticed them together before he stepped out to make his call. He was curious to hear Daisy Mae's perspective, as she had also been in their company.

Romeo extended his hand as he shifted the truck into gear, and Daisy Mae placed her tiny hand in his. Her small hand seemed delicate and fragile compared to his. Despite her petite size, Daisy Mae exuded a feisty and spirited energy.

"*Bien.* Your *mère* be relieved he be coming home. *Mais,* she be worried dat he have another heart attack."

How did she get that second part? Had Romeo's mom confided in Daisy Mae? That made him upset at himself for not keeping that close relationship with his parents. Speaking with them every week hadn't been enough. Romeo should have come home sooner.

Romeo squeezed her hand. He was also worried about his papa. The man didn't like to lie around, so keeping him down would be tricky. Could his mom do it alone? Probably not. It looked like he would be taking an extended leave to help her.

He didn't mind. It also gave him time with Daisy Mae. He wouldn't leave until her situation was resolved and she was packed up. Then again, Romeo could leave HIS for Daisy Mae and move back home. He had no idea what he'd do for a living, but he'd do anything for her.

Romeo glanced at Daisy Mae while waiting in the lengthy queue at the fast food joint. She had her hair pulled back under a ball cap, wore minimal makeup, a fitted T-shirt displaying her business name, and loose shorts. He was captivated by her. No woman, other than Daisy Mae, had ever grabbed his attention, appearing as if she had just emerged from the bayou.

Romeo leaned toward the middle of the truck. "Come here, Rocket."

Daisy Mae narrowed her eyes at him. "Why do ya call me Rocket?"

Smiling, Romeo squeezed her hand. "Come here and kiss me, then I'll tell you.

With a sly smile, she leaned toward him, and their lips touched. It was a soft, simple kiss, but one that made his libido cry for the evening date. Romeo felt a jolt as they separated at the sudden beep of a horn. Clearing his throat, he turned and pulled forward to place his order. The heat in his face made it clear that he had blushed bright red.

His companions teasingly dubbed him "Romeo" for his awkwardness around stunning women. However, tonight, he was determined to embody the true essence of that name, as she truly deserved a Romeo.

Only Daisy Mae had no idea he was playing for keeps.

Chapter Fifteen

DAISY MAE HADN'T expected to spend so much time with Steve's family, but after they returned with breakfast, Steve made her sit, and they stayed until Wayne's doctor appeared.

She had a great time with them. They laughed and listened to Steve's stories about missions gone—what he called "sideways."

Barbara briefed him on all the gossip in town so that he would know what to say or not to say around some of the town's citizens. Even Daisy Mae, who thought she knew everything that was happening in the parish, had learned a thing or two, especially about who was involved romantically with whom.

After Wayne was released, Daisy Mae and Steve accompanied the couple on their journey home. While driving to Steve's parents' house, Steve reached over and offered his hand to Daisy Mae. Without hesitation, she entwined her hand with his. At that moment, she didn't care that he would be leaving again. She simply wanted to enjoy his attention.

Since Steve's father was discharged from the hospital, would this special evening with Steve also mark the end of their romantic beginnings? Despite having no obvious obligation to stay, she longed to become the very reason he chose to remain by her side.

After finishing a light lunch, Daisy Mae's phone rang. She almost jumped for joy when she answered it.

"I can be at ya *bateau* in *une heure*," her mechanic Etienne said.

She glanced at her watch and understood there would be ample time for Etienne to repair her boat before their date. However, she had traveled with Steve, so she needed to consult with him.

"Hold on." She covered the receiver and turned to Steve, who watched her at the kitchen table. "Can ya take me back to me *bateau*? The mechanic be on his way."

Steve nodded. "I can do dat."

Talking back into the receiver, she said, "I'll see ya there, Etienne."

As Daisy Mae and Steve bid farewell to Steve's parents, they made their way to the pier, the sky painted with the warm hues of the midday sun. Despite her usual composure, Daisy Mae found herself on edge, her usually steady nerves betraying her as she contemplated broaching the topic of their evening plans. It was a rare occurrence for her to experience such unease, yet in the presence of Steve, certain moments seemed to unravel her otherwise unflappable demeanor.

As Steve parked, she said, "*Merci*. What time ya be back?"

Chuckling, Steve opened his truck door. "Rocket, I be staying."

Why was he staying? Was he staying forever? No, that couldn't be. It seemed more like he was waiting while her boat was repaired. Then again, maybe he'd stay for the night. Was she ready for that? No. Yes. She was. She'd waited a long time to be with Steve. Daisy Mae would never pass up a chance to be his, even if it were just for one night. Her heart could deal with the fallout later. It had once before and could survive again.

Coming around the front of the truck, he smiled at her. "Let's go."

Walking down the pier, Steve kept a light touch on her back. Daisy Mae tingled all over from that contact. How on earth could she handle it if he touched her intimately? She'd probably pass out from pleasure.

"Who be fixin' the *bateau*?" Steve asked, pulling her from her musings.

"Uh– Oh, Etienne Hebert. Do ya 'member him from school? I think he be in ya grade."

Steve stopped and stiffened. "Etienne. The biggest flirt in high school?"

Daisy Mae couldn't help but notice the tinge of jealousy in his voice. She knew she shouldn't be pleased by it, but something was intriguing about his reaction that she couldn't ignore. "Was he?" she asked coyly. "I only 'member him ahead of me grade." She didn't want to mention that he was still a huge flirt, but she thought Steve would find out soon.

They began walking again and reached *Seas the Day*. Etienne waited, leaning against a pylon, all sexy and as if he didn't have a care in the world.

"*Bonjour, ma chère.*" Etienne reached for Daisy Mae's hand as if to guide it to his lips.

Steve stepped forward, almost pushing her behind him. "*Bonjour*, Etienne." He held out his hand to meet the other man's. "Remember me?" he nearly growled.

Etienne stiffened. "*Mais oui*. Steve Smith. Ya home for good?"

Daisy Mae held her breath, waiting for the answer to the question she had longed to ask.

"*Non*," was his one-word reply, crushing her heart. She knew he wasn't, but she'd wanted a different answer. Would that change her wanting to sleep with him? No, she didn't think so.

Steve grabbed her hand. "We will wait up here while ya repair the engine."

Daisy Mae's blood boiled with anger. It was her beloved boat, and she refused to let anyone dictate what happened to it. With a sharp movement, she withdrew her hand from Steve's. "I be going below with ya, Etienne."

Steve grabbed her hand again, tugging her toward him. Possessive, much? "*Non*, we'll be up here." He turned them toward the bow. "Come on. I need to speak wit ya."

To avoid making a scene, Daisy Mae agreed and nodded to Etienne. "I'll be up here if ya need me."

"*Bien*." Etienne strode away.

When the mechanic was out of what Daisy Mae hoped was hearing distance, she pulled her hand away from Steve. "*Merde*! What dat be? *Seas the Day* is me *bateau*. Mine." She pointed at her chest. "Ya not come here directing what happens."

"*Resser!*"

Daisy Mae became angry when he told her to calm down. He seemed oblivious to women's feelings.

"*Resser*? *Resser*? Ya no see anything for me to calm down from—yet."

He walked too close to her. Daisy Mae caught a whiff of his divine cologne or aftershave.

His fingers gently intertwined with hers as he gazed into her eyes, creating a tender and intimate connection.

Daisy Mae tried to remind herself that she was angry with him and should not have let him touch her, but oh, how good it felt. What was the right word? Oh, yes, sensual.

Leaning his forehead to hers, he said, "I be sorry. I don't know what I be thinking. Ya be right, of course. This be your *bateau*. I was just—just jealous."

Had Steve confessed to feeling jealous? Her heart leaped in her chest. There was hope for them.

Before she could respond, he straightened and pulled her to sit, dropping one of her hands. "I hear there be a crawfish festival 'cross the pond. Want to go?"

"Now?" She couldn't think straight. What had happened?

Steve's thumb rubbed her hand in his. Each stroke sent sparks of electricity through her system.

"*Non*, Rocket. The *bateau* needs repair first."

She envisioned a lively festival as the setting for their first date, unwittingly shattering her hopes for a romantic evening of candlelight and intimacy. "Hey! Why ya call me Rocket? Ya never said."

Steve chuckled. "Ever since ya were a young girl, ya were calm *mais* quick to explode."

Daisy Mae was taken aback. Had he really said that? Feeling a surge of emotions, she swiftly pulled her hand away from his, rose to her feet, and placed both hands firmly on her hips, her mind racing with thoughts. "I do not."

Steve laughed. Laughed. He stood. "Case in point."

"I did n—" Okay, so she had gone off fast. That didn't mean she did it all the time.

"Would ya prefer I call ya something else?"

Yes and no. Yes, because it made Daisy Mae feel like Steve thought she was emotionally unsteady. No, because he'd designed a unique pet name for her.

Surprising her, he pulled her into his arms and leaned down to whisper, "How 'bouts I call ya sweetheart?"

Chapter Sixteen

ROMEO'S HEART THUMPED against his chest, each beat echoing the intensity of his emotions as he anxiously awaited Daisy Mae's response. Questioning his motives, he couldn't help but wonder why he was putting himself through this, mainly when he had already made plans to leave. Yet, with no obstacle standing between them, he strongly desired to make her his own. He intended to whisk her away with him, envisioning countless idyllic spots to dock her boat and continue her ventures into the world of charters. As he contemplated the possibilities, he couldn't help but acknowledge the allure of Baltimore's bustling harbor, a renowned tourist destination ripe with opportunities.

Daisy Mae leaned back slightly, her eyes meeting Romeo's. She gazed into them, searching for something. Romeo wasn't entirely sure what she was seeking, but he hoped she would discover it. "*Non,* I prefer Rocket."

Romeo's dreams of persuading her to join him in Baltimore were shattered. Despite the setback, he was unwavering in his determination. With no urgency to return, he could devote as much time as necessary to nurturing their relationship. He harbored the hope that his teammates, all of whom were single, would be understanding of his situation.

"Rocket, it be. Now, let's sit *et* figure out tonight."

Romeo and Daisy Mae were engrossed in lighthearted conversation and laughter while Etienne diligently worked repairing *Seas the Day*. Their camaraderie provided a welcome escape from reality as they lost themselves in each other's company.

After the mechanic finished, he told them something they had already suspected.

"Someone sabotage da *bateau*," Etienne said. "*Merde, couyon.*"

Romeo intended to use a worse word than that. He was tempted to throttle someone for touching Daisy Mae's pride and joy. The boys would be in tomorrow and would find out what was happening.

"Are you going to *une bouille d'écrevisses?*" Etienne asked.

The crawfish festival. They were, but Romeo hoped Etienne wasn't attending. Even though it was a public event, Romeo wanted Daisy Mae to himself.

"*Mais oui*," Daisy Mae said.

After Daisy Mae and Etienne settled business and the mechanic left, Romeo approached Daisy Mae. "How about dat festival? We can drive 'round or take the *bateau* over. Whichever ya prefer."

Romeo hoped she said boat so he wouldn't have to concentrate on the roadway. He wanted his focus on Daisy Mae.

"Let's take *Seas the Day*. I need to check her out before I can take her on another charter."

Romeo felt hopeful as things began to look up for him.

"I need to change first," Daisy Mae said.

Romeo appraised her and deemed her adorable as she was. But he'd learned women were picky about their looks. Only, he hadn't expected it from Rocket. "Ya look *bien*," he said, "*mais* if ya wants to change, go 'head."

"Aren't ya goin' home ta change?"

Romeo looked down at his dark, knee-length cargo shorts and matching black T-shirt. He let out a sigh of dissatisfaction. Although he was fond of his outfit, he also brought a different shirt in case he needed to change. Initially, he had intended to wear the alternative shirt in the morning, but now it seemed like it would serve its purpose.

"I be right back." After seeing her off, he quickly returned to his truck and changed his shirt. It was a gift from Brad's wife, who had mentioned that it matched his captivating hazel eyes. Knowing that women were fond of matching, he had deliberately selected it.

When he returned to the boat, he stopped when he saw Daisy Mae. Dressed to impress, she wore a short denim skirt and a tank top. Her blonde hair flowed around her toned, tanned shoulders. Her large, bright blue eyes, no longer shaded by her ballcap, drew him into her spell.

Unable to control himself, he stepped forward, put one hand behind her head, and kissed her on her plump— sans makeup—lips. Romeo meant it as a quick kiss, but she tasted so good that he reached around her sexy body and pulled her into his arms. Damn, if she didn't fit perfectly.

Daisy Mae wrapped her arms around his neck and kissed him back. She moaned, and it drove him forward.

Parting her lips, his tongue dove in, exploring her mouth, playing with her tongue, battling for control. The delight of it shot straight to his heart and groin.

Romeo had always been told that he would have a moment of clarity when he came across the right woman. True to his papa's words, that moment had finally arrived. He felt it in his bones. Now, the next step was to win her heart and make her his own.

He lifted his head. "We be going to the festival or be staying in?"

Daisy Mae's eyes were filled with longing as she gazed into his. She moistened her lips, almost undoing him.

Patience. I must be patient with Rocket.

"How 'bout we go to da festival, then come back for da night?" she asked.

Did she request his presence to spend the night with her? His cock jumped at the chance, and he pulled back from her so she didn't feel his delight. It was too early for that.

"Sounds *bien*."

As Romeo's evening unfolded, it felt like a hazy dream. His gaze was fixed on Daisy Mae, longing to articulate something so profoundly moving that she would confess her love for him. Despite understanding the improbability of this outcome, a man can still hold on to his dreams.

The fair was alive with the aroma of boiled crawfish, tender potatoes, sweet corn, and savory sausage. As they indulged in the meal, it transported him back to the comforting memories of home and the days he spent there. Though those days were past, the flavors allowed him to reminisce and savor the moments.

Romeo skillfully won two stuffed animals for Daisy Mae at the shooting booth. She chose a cute cat for the smaller prize, while for the more significant award, she picked a fierce tiger. The booth owner shooed Romeo away, recognizing his exceptional marksmanship.

As they shared laughter, they also engaged in various games, including Daisy Mae's victory in the hoop on the bottle game. As a token of affection, she presented him with a small, stuffed alligator he would treasure for the rest of his life.

As they prepared to depart, they engaged in a whimsical carnival game where players attempted to shoot water into a clown's mouth using mounted guns. A group of enthusiastic children took the game quite seriously, eagerly aiming and spraying the water.

When the bell rang to begin, Daisy Mae pushed Romeo off his stool and sprayed at the clown for the kid to her left.

"Hey," he said, jumping up and reseating himself. Seeing her plan, he turned his water gun on the clown to the kid right of him. To make things even, he jostled Daisy Mae, so she temporarily lost her aim.

"So that's how it be," she said before aiming the water gun once again.

If he could have turned the gun a full ninety degrees and hit her, he would have. Just for fun, of course.

"Come on, come on," she cheered. "We need more water," she yelled to the carnival booth owner, but he only laughed and shrugged.

Ultimately, Daisy Mae's neighbor emerged victorious, and she enthusiastically exchanged fist bumps with the triumphant child. Her carefree and joyous demeanor captivated him.

He turned to his new friend and shrugged his shoulders. "Sorry."

After the kid ran off without a word, Romeo returned to Daisy Mae as she said goodbye to her new friend.

Overall, the night had been a valuable experience. They spent time relaxing in each other's company, cherishing every moment. During the evening, they unexpectedly encountered individuals with whom Romeo hadn't crossed paths since high school, which felt like a lifetime ago.

Romeo only released Daisy Mae's hand from his grasp when they sat down to eat or engaged in a game. She didn't object, as she held on tightly to his hand.

As the boat glided closer to the shore, the sounds of the water and the distant chatter gradually faded, creating a sense of quiet anticipation. Romeo's initial nervousness began to settle, replaced by a lingering concern that perhaps she had reconsidered her decision about him staying. Had he misinterpreted her intentions, or had she genuinely changed her mind?

No matter. Romeo was staying, and he would have Daisy Mae in his– uh, her captain's bed.

Chapter Seventeen

DAISY MAE FOUND herself drawn to the idea of being intimate with Steve, but she was unsure if she was ready to take that step. Ever since she could remember, she had yearned for him, but now that an opportunity with him lay before her, nerves overwhelmed her. A profound emptiness gnawed at her core as she longed to escape, yearning to preserve his memory without facing the painful possibility of rejection.

She chose not to flee but remained steadfast, her heart yearning for Steve to reciprocate her feelings. His playful banter and subtle hints kept her guessing about the depth of his emotions. When he kissed her, every nerve in her body tingled with desire, making her wonder if it was enough for him to take her to bed tonight, leave his job, and stay with her.

No. She had made up her mind not to burden him with that request. She knew he wouldn't fulfill it, and the inevitable disappointment would cause her more significant heartache than his departure. The interaction would revolve solely around physical intimacy with no emotional connection. This would be the case if he desired to engage in sexual activity with her.

Despite the challenges she faced with her boat, including sabotage, she maintained her focus on Steve. After he finished securing the boat to the dock, she turned her attention to him, eager to discuss their next steps and plan for the rest of the evening. As he sprang back onto the boat, his intense gaze locked onto her, pulling her in so firmly that she felt as if she were gliding toward him. It was clear—he yearned for her.

"So," she paused, uncertain what to say next.

"So," he said back, smiling that smile that had to have women dropping their panties. She knew that she was ready to drop hers.

"Do ya want something to drink?"

He squinted and studied her intently. What was he hoping to discern? Could he detect her nervousness?

"*Oui*." He walked to her and stopped an arm's length away. "Do ya want to drink here and watch the sunset?"

Her limbs crackled with heat as she stood close to him, feeling the intense energy between them. She was acutely aware of his body's defined contours and the subtle prominence of his shorts. She wrestled with the idea of forgoing the drinks, but her jangling nerves craved some form of courage.

"*Bière* or water?" she asked.

"Water." He settled on a secluded bench at the back of the boat, prompting Daisy Mae's curiosity, considering two plush chairs were available. Then it dawned on her— the seating arrangement meant she had to sit beside him. She considered this a small victory.

"I be right back." Daisy Mae made her way downstairs, the creaking of the old wooden steps echoing in the silence. She opened the door of her quaint refrigerator and carefully pulled out two glistening water bottles. As she carried them, she couldn't help but notice her trembling hands. Never had she experienced such overwhelming nervousness.

She had engaged in sex a few times in the past, but it had left her feeling unfulfilled. However, she had a strong intuition that her experience with Steve would be exceptional, filled with enchantment and intense passion.

Daisy Mae took a deep breath to calm herself. She might not have to approach him after all. His bulge suggested he wanted her.

As she prepared to climb the stairs, her gaze lingered on her neatly made bed. Despite having already straightened the covers when she dressed, a sense of doubt prompted her to give it a second inspection.

She handed Steve a water bottle as she stood on the boat's deck. He acknowledged her with a nod of thanks and gestured for her to sit next to him by patting the seat. "Sit."

She nodded jerkily and then sat still as a board.

"Relax, Rocket. I no here to molest ya."

"I know dat." Just that light banter melted the steel in her back, and she turned to him. "Did ya enjoy yourself?"

Steve took a moment to glance at the array of stuffed animals they had dropped onto the deck. A wave of joy spread across his face, causing a large smile to form. "*Oui*. I did." He paused to take a refreshing sip of water, then pivoted to face her. "How 'bout you?"

They sat mere inches apart, their eyes locked in a hypnotic trance. Daisy Mae's breath hitched in anticipation as she yearned for his kiss to be so passionate that it made her forget her name. She hesitated at the thought of kissing him. In the past, she had kissed men she was dating, but in this case, they weren't dating. They were— What were they? Star-crossed lovers. Only they weren't lovers. Yet.

Raising his brows, Steve asked, "Rocket? Ya wit me?"

She shook herself out of her romantic musings, returning to the present moment, and then she smiled. "*Oui. Merci* for winning me the stuffed animals." She'd treasure them, and they'd be prominently displayed on her bed when he left. "It be a beautiful sunset."

Steve set his water down and turned serious. "I no be beating around the bush. I want ya, Daisy Mae–right now. I need to be inside ya, making ya mine…touching every inch of ya…kissing my way down ya sexy body…giving ya enough pleasure to last a lifetime."

Daisy Mae felt her throat go dry. He didn't beat around the bush. "I want ya, too," she squeaked out. Not wanting to answer him that way, she cleared her throat and said firmly, "I want ya, too, Steve."

Taking her water bottle from her, Steve set it aside. "Then git over here." His arm slithered around her waist, drawing her gently onto his lap. Right up against his hardness. And not just body hardness. Dang, he was built in all the right places.

Steve put his forehead to hers and whispered, "I be wanting ya for so long."

Really? She wanted to ask how long, but that wasn't appropriate now. "I be wanting ya since I knew what want was."

"Oh, Rocket." Their lips collided in an intense, passionate kiss. She wrapped her arms around his neck and instinctively shifted in his lap, deepening the embrace. She couldn't get close enough.

With their tongues at play, Daisy Mae moaned her pleasure. Finally, she'd have the love of her life in her bed. That niggling doubt of doing this and then his leaving tried to surface, but she squashed it with her need for this man. It rivaled the love of her boat.

When their lips parted, Steve let out a long sigh. "Wow."

Wow, indeed. Her toes had curled on that one.

"Let's go below," he suggested.

She was quick to act, graceful as she slipped off his lap and confidently led the way, her senses heightened by the closeness of his presence. She couldn't shake the feeling that this bayou sunset would forever be etched in her memory.

Chapter Eighteen

ROMEO WAS SURE he was dreaming. Before him stood Daisy Mae with longing eyes, offering herself to him. He never dared to believe that this day would ever come. After resisting the temptation all those years ago, Romeo never thought he would reencounter her. Although he intended to visit his family at some point, he was determined to stay away from her. His heart could not cope with Daisy Mae being romantically involved with another man—married with three-plus children.

As they reached below deck, Daisy Mae paused, holding a hand up. "Wait a second," she said, disappearing inside. After a moment, she emerged again, having flicked on a pair of fans that she had seemingly charged earlier. "I believe"—she removed her tank top to reveal a strapless lavender lacy bra—"it's gonna get hot in here tonight."

Romeo stood paralyzed, his mind filled with questions about when and how he had relinquished control of the night. "Hold up there, swee— Rocket." He strolled into the tiny cabin. "That be my job to undress ya." He needed to regain the advantage once more. This was his ultimate dream realized—dammit.

She slipped off her shoes, and he followed suit.

"There be no 'jobs' here, but if ya wanna undress me,"—with a coy smile, she traced a finger down the middle of her chest, sending all his blood to his groin, not that most of it wasn't there already—"come here, Romeo."

Taken aback by the fact that she had referred to him as Romeo, he was momentarily thrown off balance, almost faltering in his step. He wasn't sure he liked it from her. It wasn't that she was a woman. They employed female agents who affectionately referred to him as "Romeo," but he longed to hear his real name, "Steve." At times, he found himself yearning for his true identity.

"Are ya gonna remain standing dere?" she inquired, her tone filled with impatience.

Romeo cleared his throat. "Call me Steve, not Romeo, if you please."

Daisy Mae cocked her head in a thoughtful gesture. "If it be important to ya, *oui*."

Nodding, he stepped to her. "It be. Now, about dis lacy contraption…." His fingers tingled with the need to touch her. Reaching up, he gently cupped both her breasts as if weighing them. Perfection. "I do believe," he said, then spun her around, "this needs ta come off." He effortlessly unhooked her bra, trailing kisses down the side of her neck and shoulder. She tasted and smelled like what he expected heaven would be like.

Romeo pulled her back to his chest, then reached around and touched her breasts again, continuing the assault on her neck and shoulder. "Mmm, ya taste good.

Smell even better," he muttered between trailing wet kisses.

"Steve, quit teasing me." She moaned loudly. "I be ready."

He stilled. Did she think he was a "wham-bam, thank you, ma'am" kind of guy? Had that been her experience with men? He may not have had the most practice, but he knew how to please a woman. And he would pleasure this woman all night.

Romeo gently guided her to turn around and meet his gaze by placing his hand under her chin and tilting it towards him. "Rocket, dere be no need to rush this. We got all night."

Her intense gaze revealed the answer he sought. She longed for him as much as he did for her. Not that he'd doubted it with her getting half-naked. At times, he found that women tended to perplex him with their actions and words.

"Let's take dis slow and easy," he said, touching her cheeks and gently cupping her face. "*Mais*, kiss me."

Romeo bent down to match Daisy Mae's height, and she stood on her toes to kiss him. Once they molded together, warmth suffused Romeo's body. It was more potent than anything he'd ever felt with a woman. He had no idea if he'd survive when he was actually inside her.

At that, his cock twitched, ready for action. He broke the kiss, reached down, and adjusted himself. He had always been taught to let ladies go first, though he doubted whether his mother's lesson had been intended to apply to sexual situations. So, he found the zipper on the back of her skirt and removed the garment, letting it pool to the floor at her feet.

Mon Dieu! She wore a lavender lacy thing, and he thought—he spun her again—yep, thong. He believed she wore it for him, and it wasn't her everyday wear. Either way, he didn't care at that moment. All he knew was that she had one fine, luscious ass.

Daisy Mae glanced back over her shoulder with a mischievous smile and playfully asked, "Do ya like what ya see?"

Merde, I do. Quirking his lip, he said, "It'll suffice."

She spun around and swatted him on the chest. "Why ya—"

Romeo's mouth covered hers, breaking off her words. He loved to see her hot-blooded. As their tongues dueled and danced, he slipped off her panties, grabbed her butt, and pulled her against his rigid cock. One that had to be released soon from the confines of his shorts.

Gently pulling away from the kiss, he whispered between heavy breaths, "Daisy Mae, I need ya."

"I need ya, too, Steve." She sounded more winded than he did, and he wasn't sure that was possible.

He removed his shirt and shorts in nearly one swift motion.

With the confidence of a man who'd bedded millions of women but only had bedded a few, he walked her back until her knees met the edge of her bed, and she fell back onto the mattress. "Finally," he said as he knelt before her, "I've got ya where I want ya."

"Steve, get ya ass up here. I need ya inside me, now."

"Sorry, Rocket, I be where I'm supposed to be now." He parted her legs and kissed the inside of her thighs before he looked at her womanly center. Damn, she was pretty and pink and—he touched a finger to her wet folds

—ready for him. But he wasn't prepared. Well, he was, but not entirely. He wouldn't allow himself to come before he gave her pleasure.

Teasing her, he kissed his way from the inside of her thigh to her center. He licked her folds and nibbled at her nub, listening to her moan and gasp. Those little noises drove his need to explore and conquer all of her, to know every inch of *his* woman.

Yeah, he knew she was *his* woman. He wouldn't try to hide that fact like some of his brethren did when they fell in love.

Tasting ambrosia, he continued his assault on her center while he slipped a finger inside her heat. *Mon Dieu!* He was about to come himself.

But, he held himself in check, waiting until his efforts yielded her tensing, lifting her hips, and shuddering to cry out his name. Working her nub, he extended her climax until she cried, "No more."

"Sorry, *mon amour*, dere be lots more." He froze, wondering if she'd caught he'd just called her "his love." When she only closed her eyes with a sated smile, he breathed. He'd have to be more careful until the time was right.

He stood, dropped his briefs, reached for his shorts, and removed the condom he'd placed in a pocket, praying the night went his way. "Scoot up on dat there bed."

His hands shook while Daisy Mae watched him put the condom on his dick. He struggled to maintain his composure even though the night had just begun.

"Why didn't I get a turn?" she asked.

Oui, like I can handle that right now. He was so hypersensitive to her touch that he'd come if she brushed the head of his cock. "Next time."

The smile on her face conveyed her desire for the next time, boosting his confidence.

Romeo gazed at her beautiful face while he slid over her, resting on his elbows. "Ya be everything I always wanted in a woman."

"*Oui*, ya be everything I always wanted in a man."

Romeo slid his body between her legs, feeling the heat radiate from her body.

"Where does dat leave us, Steve?"

"Right now? In dis bed, enjoying the hell out of each other. Driving each other 'til we be so aware of our heartbeats that we feel like we be beating as one."

"*Oui*," she breathed, then moaned when he leaned over and kissed below her earlobe. "Ya be good wit words."

He nibbled his way down her neck toward her breast. "Those no be just words. I want it all." When he reached her nipple, he took it in his mouth, flicking the peak with his tongue.

Daisy Mae moaned, running her hands through Romeo's hair and wrapping her legs around his, pulling him tight to her core. "Steve, quit torturing me."

Reaching down, Romeo found what he'd already known, slick with her release—she was more than ready for him. He guided his cock to her opening and slowly slid in. Not to brag, but he was a relatively large man, not huge, but larger than most, and she was tiny and tight. *Mon Dieu!* She was tight.

Romeo groaned and almost bit his tongue to keep from coming right then and there. He wasn't even entirely inside her, and he was ready to blow his wad. "*Merde*, Daisy Mae, ya feel so good. I no sure I be able to last long."

"Ya be speaking to the choir. I be almost ready again as ya fill me. Each new thrust brings me closer and closer to da summit."

Done with words—actually, unable to speak any longer because his smaller head had taken control—he slid into the hilt and stopped. Sighing with a pleasure he'd never imagined, Romeo didn't want to move. He could remain joined like this forever. Did life get any sweeter or perfect than this?

Unfortunately, Rocket couldn't be still. She squirmed underneath him. So, he withdrew and thrust again. This would be his woman for all eternity. He would make it known by showing her how much he loved and cared for her.

Daisy Mae adjusted her legs around him and shifted. Before he knew what had happened, she flipped them over. "Ya be going too slow," she said, sitting up on him. "We can go slow later."

Joy infused his heart. He couldn't agree more. Reaching up to her hips, he helped her control the rhythm until beads of sweat glistened on their bodies.

Romeo grabbed her ass and kept her tight against him with each thrust, ensuring she took him as deeply as possible. Having his hands on her ass reaffirmed his thoughts of how perfectly it was shaped.

When she sat up and deepened their connection, Romeo felt the tingle run down his spine and then the surge and tightness in his balls. To ensure she came before he did, he reached down and rubbed her clit. He'd always been a considerate, albeit inexperienced, lover, guaranteeing the women he bedded came once. He'd never cared for twice until now with Daisy Mae.

"I be coming," she breathed.

Romeo had never heard sweeter words. "Fly for me, Rocket."

When she shuddered, cried his name, and then collapsed forward, Steve thrust twice more before groaning, feeling euphoric and exhausted in the same instance. His orgasm had been the strongest he'd ever experienced. It'd been the only one where his heart was connected.

He hadn't lied about feeling their heartbeats as one. As hers beat against his, where she'd collapsed onto him, he felt the syncing of their love.

Chapter Nineteen

ROMEO WAS UNCERTAIN, wondering if he would fully recover from his intense night with Daisy Mae. It had been a truly magnificent and highly charged experience, filled with sensual and unforgettable moments. Yet, as he reflected on the encounter, one burning question lingered: Would he dare to embark on such an exhilarating journey again? *Mais oui*! He planned to be with Daisy Mae before he departed, hoping that she might decide to accompany him to Maryland.

Standing on the wooden deck with a cup of steaming coffee in hand, Romeo gazed intently at the tranquil sight of the dock, its weathered planks bathed in the warm glow of the morning sun. The boys were expected to arrive soon, and he desired to ensure that Daisy Mae was already dressed before their arrival. He dreaded the thought of her unintentionally encountering them while minimally clothed, under the impression that they were alone.

It would have been idyllic for them to have some alone time until he had to depart. His departure was held up by the urgent need to unravel the mystery of what Daisy Mae had become entangled in, which had caused her distress.

Before she even spoke, Romeo was suddenly aware of her presence behind him. It wasn't a feeling of danger that made the hairs on the back of his neck stand up, but rather a zinging desire that went straight to his heart and dick.

He cautiously blew on the steaming coffee, savoring the rich aroma before taking a careful sip. As he swallowed the hot brew, he turned to face the love of his life. "Good morning, Rocket," he greeted affectionately. It still stung that she didn't respond well to "sweetheart," but he was determined to find the right words to express his feelings.

She blushed, her eyes averted as she softly murmured, "Good morning."

Merde. Her demeanor exuded preciousness, yet her nervousness left him wondering if it was simply due to her nerves or a manifestation of regret. He desperately hoped that it was not the latter.

"Thank ya for making dis coffee," she appreciatively expressed as she brought the cup to her lips and took a delicate sip.

"Let's sit. I be watching for the guys."

"Do ya think they be showing up dis early?" She settled in the commanding captain's chair, creating distance between them. It was an unsettling prospect.

"I be surprised they not be on the deck waiting for us." He positioned himself close to her instead of taking a seat, determined not to let any distance come between them. They had crossed a significant threshold the previous night and officially became a couple. It wouldn't be long before she recognized this as well.

"What be their names again?"

"Grits and Casper."

"Funny names. Is it like ya Romeo name?" She hadn't called him that again after he'd asked her to call him Steve. "What be their real names?"

Romeo paused for a moment, carefully contemplating the situation. He was still determining how Rob Grimes and Ash McNabb would react if she were to refer to them by their actual names. Specific agents, particularly those with a background in special operations like Grits and Casper, were particular about using their names. Ultimately, he caved, "Rob Grimes and Ash McNabb."

Last night, Romeo and Daisy Mae's conversation left an unresolved issue hanging in the air. They had expressed being everything the other had ever envisioned in a partner. Romeo pondered how to broach the topic without overwhelming Daisy Mae and pressuring her to be constantly close to him. Ultimately, he resigned himself to his usual approach of blurting things out.

"Rocket, last night—"

"Is dat them?" Daisy Mae stood, pointing up the dock at the two men striding their way.

Of fucking course, it be them. Perfect timing and all. "That be dem," he bit out.

Daisy Mae paused, standing just a few feet away from him. As he watched her, he couldn't help but wonder if she had moved closer to him. At that moment, his heart yearned for her to see him as the source of her strength.

"Romeo, wherefore art thou Romeo?" Casper called. The *couyon*. Romeo heard that all the fucking time. It was old.

Romeo placed his coffee on the small table and addressed his teammates, remarking, "That be as funny as the last million times ya said it." As he extended his hand for a quick handshake, he introduced *his* woman. "Grits, Casper, I'd like ya to meet Daisy Mae. She be the person we be here to help."

Grits casually checked the time on his watch, a bemused expression crossing his face. Romeo figured Grits had realized he'd clearly spent the night with her. Romeo dismissed the situation as inconsequential despite his friends' interest, confident that the truth would inevitably come to light.

Casper extended his hand in a friendly gesture. "It's a pleasure to make your acquaintance, ma'am. My name is Casper."

"I shiver at da thought of encountering ghosts," she admitted with a nervous laugh.

Romeo offered a comforting smile in response to her comment.

She inquired, "Are ya Ash or Rob?"

The men looked at Romeo as if to say, "What the fuck?"

They turned back. "I'm Ash, ma'am."

Daisy Mae nodded. "Then I'll call you Ash. And, ya be Rob?"

Nodding in acknowledgment, Grits extended his hand and firmly clasped hers, holding on longer than Romeo found agreeable. A low, audible growl escaped from Romeo, clearly revealing his displeasure, while the boys around them merely grinned. The smug fuckers.

"Did ya get checked into a hotel?"

Grits replied, "We discovered a B&B in town. We hoped to have breakfast elsewhere but weren't sure what would be open."

"Duke's be the spot," Daisy Mae declared with a smile. "Just let me fetch my purse." With that, she headed down below deck.

Grits turned on him. "What the fuck, Romeo? She's our client."

"No, she's not. I be. I hired ya to help me find out who is screwing with her. So get over it. And, Grits, try that shit again, and I'll punch ya in the face." He intentionally held Daisy Mae's hand for an extended period, aiming to provoke a reaction from Romeo. Despite being the leader of Bravo team, Romeo refused to tolerate it.

Grits put his hands up, palms out. "Okay. I was testing the waters between you two. Now I know. She seems nice. Don't break her fucking heart."

"I don't plan to. She be coming with me?"

"Oh? I be?"

Merde. Romeo spun. "Yeah, ya be riding with me. The boys have transportation."

Doubt colored Daisy Mae's expression as she narrowed her eyes at him, her skepticism evident. She was going to see right through him—he could feel it.

Daisy Mae shrugged. "*Oui*," she ultimately said.

Merde. He knew he had to be careful. While he might mention to the others that she was joining him in Baltimore, Daisy Mae wasn't quite prepared to hear that yet. He realized that he still needed to persuade her further.

During the journey to Duke's, Daisy Mae inquired, "Why we no ride together? There be plenty of room wit the backseat of da truck."

Why? Why? Why? Think faster, brain. "Because dey plan to start their investigation now. Didn't ya say ya brothers wanted to return to the island today?"

Daisy Mae nodded. "*Oui*, but I thought ya friends were going too."

"They be, but you and I must prepare the *bateau*. I think we ate what was left of the food and drank all the water, trying to rehydrate." He turned and winked at her.

"*Mais*, I see where ya be going with dis." She turned to him, putting her knee on the seat. He glanced at her from the driver's seat.

"What?"

"Well, ya be enjoying it all again. Being here around the *bateau* and water, ya be visiting ya parents more often."

He got an "and me" but let it go. "That sounds *bien*."

Even though he watched the road, he felt her eyes boring into his as if trying to mind-meld. "What, Rocket?"

"Do ya think I be in some danger? Or do ya think someone be just fucking wit me?"

Romeo pulled into a spot at Duke's and parked the truck. He turned to her. "Ya be in some coil, that be for sure. The question be whether it be your coil or one ya *frères* brought ya way."

"Me *frères*?" she asked, stunned. "What do dey have to do wit dis?"

"It either be da map or someone wants ya business?"

"How can ya know that? Ya only been here for a few days."

He had a gut feeling that he was right about this. "It might not be, but those be my professional guesses. The boys will determine the problem, and we'll resolve it."

"Do we include me?"

He was determined not to let her put herself in any more danger. However, he knew she might withdraw from the situation or convince others to let her participate. He believed it was in her best interest to stay by his side. "Can ya stay by me side through dis?"

With pleading eyes, she asked, "Only through dis?"

"That be a talk for another time. The boys be waiting. Let's get some breakfast. Some insatiable woman helped me work up an appetite dis morning." Tension hung heavy in the air as he leaned over to kiss her. She hesitated, and his heart cracked with uncertainty. Then, finally, she leaned in and kissed him. It wasn't a passionate or romantic kiss but held more profound, unspoken significance.

He could work with that.

Chapter Twenty

AT DUKE'S, DAISY Mae contemplated whether she'd run into high school with the prank Ash and Rob told her they'd played on Steve. Her poor Romeo. No, she still couldn't call him that, especially not after their night together.

Rob recounted a time when Steve was assisting another agent. "Apparently, he decided to go horseback riding without wearing any underwear. Quite a hilarious mistake."

Steve let out a frustrated growl. "It be because someone done stolen all of my underwear," he said, irritation lacing his words.

Rob and Ash didn't contain their laughter, filling the room with their hearty guffaws. As they shared this moment, she couldn't help but notice the subtle twitch at the corners of Steve's mouth, indicating his attempt to conceal his amusement with a smile.

Daisy Mae was utterly taken aback by the story they had just shared with her. Did they genuinely believe she needed to know that he had gone commando? Of course, they probably assumed the two were lovers.

The idea of labeling herself and Steve as "lovers" had always seemed like a distant dream to her.

"Sorry, Daisy Mae." Ash gave her a wide, bright smile. "Romeo is too easy and fun to pick on."

Daisy Mae hesitated for a moment before speaking up. "I think," she said while trying to remain composed, "that ya be nothing but a bunch of high school kids."

They immediately sobered.

Steve touched her arm, and her body flushed with heat. "No need to worry. I got the guys back for what dey did. It all be in good fun."

"Anyhow," Rob said, putting down his fork after cleaning his plate, "let's talk about why we're here."

At Duke's, breakfast was a hearty spread featuring eggs, bacon, sausage, grits, pancakes, and biscuits. Every patron received this substantial meal, whether they desired it all or not. While not overwhelming, it was still more than Daisy Mae could finish.

"Somebody be bothering Daisy Mae. There be the shooting—"

"Shooting?" Rob echoed.

Steve turned to her. "You be there for it all. Go ahead."

That made Daisy Mae remember Steve disarming her, and she wanted to slug him. "A *bateau* followed us."

Rob and Ash appeared confused, so she clarified, "Boat for you *couyons*." She didn't explain that one for them.

"While the guys be on the island, the *bateau* went by and sprayed me *bateau* with bullets. Dey mostly missed, so dey came around again. Steve be there the second time."

"Steve?" Ash queried with his brows raised.

"I like it better than that Romeo you *couyons* call him." Daisy Mae placed her napkin beside her half-full plate. "Excuse me. I need the ladies' room."

She rose to her feet, and to her surprise, all the men at the table rose too, creating a peculiar sight given their diverse origins. Daisy Mae acknowledged them with a nod before making a swift departure.

Her emotions were in turmoil, and her hands shook uncontrollably. As she recalled the moment she was shot at, she was struck by the stark realization of how dangerous the situation had been. She'd been madder than a hornet caught in a jar then. However, she craved comfort but couldn't seek it, as Steve's friends were present.

In the women's restroom, Daisy Mae stood at the sink. The high humidity had caused her ponytail to frizz, making it an unbecoming mess under her ballcap. She tried to tame it with water from the sink and then splashed some on her face, feeling refreshed.

Knowing she had their support, she finally had the courage to tell them everything. Steve might be upset, but that was unavoidable.

Daisy Mae emerged from the restroom and noticed the men engaged in deep conversation. When she approached, they fell silent. She couldn't help but wonder if it had something to do with her.

Her steps faltered. Would Steve disclose their night together? It was one thing that they might assume the two were together, but to know for sure, and the specifics….

Embarrassed and alarmed, she quickly pivoted and hurried back to the restroom.

Ash swiftly maneuvered in front of her. Concern etched on his face. "What's wrong? We're truly sorry if anything we said offended you."

With his cute, bleached-blond hair, Ash appeared more like a surfer than a special agent. If her memory served her right, his background included experience as a paramedic, Green Beret, Delta Force, and HIS. She didn't fully comprehend the nature of the military roles, but it was evident that the guys were proud of Ash's diverse and prestigious positions.

Daisy Mae gazed up at him. "I be fine. I just forgot to wash me hands," she fibbed.

"Casper," Steve said beside her, "let her be."

The blond god nodded and returned to the table.

"You be okay?" Steve asked. He positioned himself directly in front of her, creating a barrier between her and the safety of the ladies' room. Although she didn't feel unsafe, she wasn't emotionally prepared to revisit the past. The weight of everything that had transpired was beginning to bear down heavily on her.

She knew she couldn't avoid it any longer; she had to gather her courage and confront the situation. Running away was no longer an option. As Steve gently lifted her chin with his fingertips, she felt a rush of emotions surging through her. Looking into his eyes, she found them glistening with raw desire, which sent a jolt through her heart, causing it to skip a beat. She wanted to grab and pull him into the ladies' room, then ravage his body.

"I be fine," she said instead. "I like the camaraderie ya teammates be havin'." The inane talk helped tone down the heat that flushed her body at his touch and intense gaze.

"I be worried we'd said something to upset ya. The last thing I want to do is be upsetting ya."

Then, please don't leave me after this is resolved, she wanted to say but couldn't bring herself to voice it out loud. "*Non*. I be interrupting ya conversation, so I thought I would give ya more time."

Her strength began to return as they stood facing each other, his hand gently lifting her chin to meet his gaze. Despite her lingering fear of the past events, she acknowledged they were irreversible. Resolute, she realized that she couldn't alter the past, but she was determined to move forward and bring those responsible for causing her harm to justice.

Courage restored, she nodded. "I be fine."

With a cautious look, he lowered his hand and guided her to the table. The plates had been cleared, and drinks had been replenished. Rob was diligently taking notes in a small, weathered notebook, furrowing his brows in concentration, while Ash meticulously studied a detailed waterways map. Their intense focus reflected their deep involvement in whatever task lay before them.

"All right, just to make sure I understand," Rob affirmed. "You're saying that you were shot at and that someone also sabotaged your boat. And our current suspects are a rival boat owner and a big-time treasure hunter?"

"I no be narrow it down to just dem," Steve said. "It could be anyone."

"I get that, Romeo. I'm going with leads to follow first. You know the drill," Rob said.

Ash pushed the map over to Daisy Mae. "Is this the island?"

He managed to pinpoint its location with such speed. Despite being just a tiny speck on the map, it was incredibly easy to overlook it amidst all the other markings and details. She nodded. "*Oui*."

"Daisy Mae," Rob asked, "is there anything else you want to add?"

She rubbed her hands together under the table. It was now or never. "*Oui*, there be more."

"What the fuck?" Steve yelled, just as she'd expected he would.

Daisy Mae should have told him sooner.

Chapter Twenty-One

ROMEO SEETHED WITH frustration upon learning that Daisy Mae had concealed a dangerous secret. He felt a pang of anguish, realizing his absence had left her vulnerable and unable to shield her from harm. Impatient, he leaned closer to her. "Go 'head."

"Well," she said, her voice quivering slightly as she wet her lips, a telltale sign of nervousness. "There be a note left on me *bateau* the morning we went out with me *frères*."

"What kind of note?" he growled through clenched teeth, the frustration evident in his voice. Why hadn't she informed him? He had made it clear that he would always be there to protect her.

Daisy Mae shrugged. "At the time, I no thought much 'bout it."

Grits inquired, maintaining composure in a way that Romeo wouldn't have. "What did it say?"

"Something like 'Leave the treasure alone or die.'"

"Where is this note?" Grits asked. "Do you still have it?"

Daisy Mae shook her head. "*Non*. I crumpled it up and tossed it."

Romeo's hand moved slowly and deliberately as he wiped his palm across his face. A sense of relief washed over him as he realized it was just a note, but the content of the message left a sour feeling in his gut. While he was around, no one would "or die." "Why did ya no tell me? We could've gotten prints or DNA from it, and this would be resolved."

Her back stiffened, indicating that he had said the wrong thing. "*Mais*, 'cuse me, Mr. Special Agent Man, I took it as a jest. It be before the bullets flew, and I'd forgotten 'bout it by then."

His pride was wounded, and he let out a heavy sigh, causing his chest to rise and fall pronouncedly.

"Is there anything else?" Grits asked, eyeing her curiously.

"*N— Non*."

Romeo caught that stutter.

"Daisy Mae?" Grits said in a question. "We need to know everything."

She fidgeted. "*Mais*, someone broke into me home the first night we went out. They tore up me office, but I cleaned it up. Nothing be missing."

The men groaned almost simultaneously. It was another opportunity to eliminate prints and DNA, but it was done. Romeo wouldn't criticize her for it. She hadn't realized that every aspect was intricately intertwined. Despite receiving a menacing note, being targeted with gunfire, and experiencing a break-in at her home all in one day, she still failed to recognize the seriousness of the situation. What had her life been like while he'd been away that she'd brush these things off as she had?

"Well," Casper said, "someone is definitely after this treasure and doesn't want Daisy Mae taking the twins out for it. Which reminds me, we need to meet these twins and see if they've had any threatening notes or break-ins."

Romeo stared. He had never witnessed Casper string together so many words in one go. The team's ghost was known for his brevity, so when he did choose to speak, it always carried weight and significance.

"Right," Grits agreed. "Daisy Mae, Romeo, when can we meet the twins?"

"They be here now," Daisy Mae said. "This be their bar, and dey be waiting for me to go out again."

"Fantastic," Grits exclaimed. "Could you please make the introductions for us? It's important that we meet with them before you leave."

"*Mais oui.*" Daisy Mae stood, leading the men to the bar. "JP, would ya have Pierre come out? There be people I want ya to meet."

After introducing Grits and Casper to her brothers, the men requested privacy for a discussion, leaving Romeo and Daisy Mae together.

He cleared his throat with a slight raspy sound, breaking the silence. "Would ya like another cup of coffee?" he inquired, a hint of warmth in his voice.

Daisy Mae shook her head, her blonde ponytail swaying gently, as she replied, "I be good. I need to prepare me *bateau.*"

Romeo gazed across the room, where four men were engaged in an animated discussion. He acknowledged Grits's likely advice to avoid going out until the situation was resolved. However, Romeo knew that Daisy Mae and the obstinate twins were unlikely to comply with such a directive. Or, the twins were consumed by greed and showed no concern for their sister's safety. That one sat uncomfortably in his crawl. "Let's go."

Romeo guided them away from the bar, his hand gently resting on her lower back. With that subtle touch, waves of passion surged through him. He had to have her again. His first task was to solve a significant problem that proved to be more serious than anticipated. The pressing question on his mind was, "What comes next?"

After leaving the bar, Romeo stopped and asked Daisy Mae to do the same. "Daisy Mae, I worry dat this be bigger than we thought."

Her eyes widened in what he thought was fear. "Can dey handle it?"

Indeed, they could do it, but they required her to approach it more seriously. It appeared that someone was intent on causing her harm or preventing her from reaching the island. At least, that's what they presumed was the motive behind the actions. It had started that fateful morning of the first treasure-hunting excursion.

Romeo nodded. "*Mais oui*, dey can handle it. Unlike me, their focus be on ya safety."

Daisy Mae's brows furrowed. "Why not yours?"

"Because," he said, moving closer, "I can't keep me eyes off ya." Reaching out, he pulled her into his arms. "I want ya, Daisy Mae Robichoux."

Wrapping her arms around his neck, she smiled coyly. "Ya do? How much do ya want me?"

"Enough that I could take ya right here in front of God and all of Duke's."

Daisy Mae looked around. "How about we sneak back to me *bateau* and have a quickie?"

His love for his woman knew no bounds. This thought reverberated through his mind with unwavering clarity. Leaning in, his warm and tender lips embraced her in a possessive kiss, a silent declaration of his ownership. His blood rushed south with lightning speed, leaving him a bit light-headed. Damn, he needed this woman in his life. He had to persuade Daisy Mae to relocate with him.

"Gross," JP said, walking up to them.

"Get a room," Pierre said.

Romeo reluctantly broke the kiss, his breathing heavy and labored, and he noticed the blush spreading across Daisy Mae's cheeks before he turned his attention to the men.

"Real mature," Romeo said with disdain as he slipped his hand down to hold Daisy Mae's. He defiantly looked at Grits and Casper. Let them tell him that he couldn't do the job. "What be the verdict?"

"They've also had threats and break-ins," Grits said grimly.

Merde. Why would this family choose to keep these things from him? Was it possible that they believed he was just there for amusement? Of course, he hadn't disclosed to them that his purpose for being there was to safeguard Daisy Mae so he could somewhat understand their actions.

"What be the plan?" Romeo asked.

Grits stretched his neck side to side. "We strongly recommend taking a day's break from treasure-hunting and going out on the boat. We have a few crucial things to check out first. We're worried about what will happen next—because there will be a next."

In moments, they grasped the grim reality of what was "next." The dock trembled violently as a colossal explosion tore through the air, engulfing the boat, *Seas the Day*, in a fierce inferno.

Chapter Twenty-Two

DAISY MAE STOOD frozen, her heart heavy with disbelief as she watched her boat—the lifeline of her business and the embodiment of their family legacy—vanish before her eyes in an instant. Behind her, she registered Duke's emptying of patrons.

Mario Xenos stopped beside her. *"Mon Dieu!"*

In a fleeting, frozen moment, she bolted down the dock, her name echoing behind her, yet its meaning eluding her grasp. The dock had to be evacuated quickly to prevent the fire from spreading further. Luckily, there were no boats near hers that the explosion should significantly impact, but they would take no chances.

Chaos and panic took over as boat captains frantically worked to launch their vessels while other residents and crew joined forces to help extinguish the raging flames. The volunteer fire department's response time was not ideal, leaving the task of rescuing the wooden dock in their hands. If fortune favored her, she might be able to rescue a portion of her boat and personal belongings.

After enduring hours of strenuous, gritty labor, a sense of controlled chaos gradually gave way to order. Through the collective effort, they managed to preserve most of the dock—enough to allow the boats to return despite being positioned closer to each other than before. Regrettably, her boat had not been rescued. A handful of her possessions had drifted in the water before a compassionate fisherman retrieved them for her.

Daisy Mae was consumed by her overwhelming sorrow when suddenly, she was enveloped in the reassuring embrace of solid and supportive arms. His intoxicating scent and the lingering smokey aroma enveloped her senses as she embraced him, longing for the morning when she hadn't left his side.

Now, faced with the dilemma, she pondered her options. The insurance companies in these parts had a reputation for underpaying the value of a boat, leaving her uncertain if she would receive enough to purchase a replacement. She had set aside a substantial amount of money from her savings, allowing her to make a sizable down payment. However, she was hesitant to take out a new loan. Her parents had fully paid off her boat, which had been their last gift to her.

Tears streamed down her sooty face. Things didn't get any more real than this. Although, the gunshots had been pretty real. Despite her efforts to maintain her strength and self-sufficiency, the destruction of her boat was a setback she found exceedingly challenging to bear.

"You," Mario said beside her, anger in his voice.

Daisy Mae gently disengaged from Steve's embrace and pivoted to face her adversary. Anticipating his potential outburst, she preempted him, saying, "Don't start today, Mario. I no be in the mood."

"It be ya fault we lose da dock."

The situation had reached its breaking point. It was unquestionably not her fault. An asshole had callously destroyed her boat. Fuming with anger she hadn't felt in ages, she let her fury loose on Mario. With a finger jabbing into his massive chest, she seethed, "I said don't start. I no blow up me *bateau*, ya— ya *couyon*. Ya be a suspect as far as I be concerned." She turned to Steve. "Can't ya detain him or something?"

Steve stood with a firm and composed posture. His arms confidently crossed over his chest as he observed the show. What was wrong with men? Wasn't he supposed to support and protect her? Isn't that what couples did? Well, they weren't a couple, just lovers—actually, a one-night stand.

"*Moi*?" Mario asked, looking between her and Steve. "I no do anyting wrong." He pointed at Daisy Mae. "She be stubborn as a goat."

With a surge of frustration, she drew her arm back, preparing to unleash a decisive blow to Mario's jaw. However, before her fist could make contact, someone swiftly intercepted, gripping her arm and arresting its forward trajectory. Damn, Steve. Now, he interferes.

"That be enough," Steve said, holding her arm, "both of ya."

"*Mais*, he—"

"I know what he said, sweetheart."

Before she could respond to either his siding with Mario or calling her sweetheart, his buddies stepped forward.

"Introduce us, Daisy Mae," Rob said with Ash at his side.

Daisy Mae shot a piercing glare at the man. Was he serious about going for formality after someone blew up her boat while her rival pilot's boat miraculously survived? Enough was enough. "Introduce yourself. I be done with dat *couyon*." She walked away. Let them figure it out. She was going to talk to Alice.

Alice had diligently collected statements from witnesses until she could sit down with Daisy Mae and delve into the details of what had transpired over a casual drink at Duke's, and that time had finally arrived. Daisy Mae had had enough of men for the day.

Someone grabbed her arm and pulled her to a stop, and without looking back, she knew it was Steve.

"Daisy Mae," Steve said, "stop. I be wanting to talk wit you."

Not wanting to deny the stupid man anything, she halted and turned. "*Oui*?" What would be so profound now? He wouldn't hold Mario or interrogate him. What good was he?

As her cheeks warmed with embarrassment, she couldn't help but think back to the events of the previous evening and what he was capable of.

"If ya calm down—"

Those were the wrong words to say to a woman, especially now. "Calm down? Calm down? I show ya calm down." As she swiftly pivoted away from him, she entered Duke's. Inside, she spotted Alice at a table, where two frosted beers glistened in the dim light. She joined her friend at the table with a quick stride, ready to unwind after a terrible morning. When Steve approached the table, she held up a hand to stop him, "*Non*. This be me interview wit the police. I no need ya here."

Hesitantly, as if suddenly comprehending his mistake, he uttered, "Okay, but I be here when ya finish. We not be done by a long shot, Daisy Mae."

The intensity of their relationship was overwhelming her. She felt the need to take some time to unwind and reflect on the current state of her life.

"Here." Alice pushed a cold glass of beer. "Drink up. It sounds like ya be needing it."

Did she ever! "*Merci*." After taking a long drink of the brew, she sat the glass down, condensation slipping down her fingers. "I did need dat."

"I sure be sorry about ya *bateau*." Alice flipped open the small notepad on the table.

Daisy Mae often marveled at how Alice could fit all her notes in such a small notebook, but it was standard issue for the sheriff's department, and her friend had become accustomed to its compact size. "It no be ya fault."

"*Mais*," Alice said, "let's see if we can find out who be at fault."

"*Oui*. What do ya have?" Daisy Mae eagerly anticipated that Alice's inquiries to others had unearthed profound insights.

"I be sorry to say—nothing."

"Nothing? How could ya be having nothing?" Daisy Mae's fury was unleashed. "We have Mario, and if dat not be enough, Antoine still thinks me *frères* stole his map. One of dem had to have done it. And Mario be right here. He coulda set off an explosion and ensured his *bateau* be safe." Wasn't it coincidental that his boat was parked further from hers than usual? Hmm.

"Daisy Mae," Alice said calmly, "I not be done investigating. I got nothing from anyone out dere today. I plan to speak wit Mario, Antoinne, and everyone else I can. The sheriff no be happy about having something explode in his parish, especially after shots were fired at that same *bateau*. I be pressed to solve it fast."

"What about ya other cases? Ya be having a big load already." Daisy Mae rubbed her finger over the rim of her glass, trying to comprehend it all.

"The sheriff give dem to someone else. Now, I be completely devoted to dis case."

With the help of her friend and Steve's friends, she anticipated that this "situation" would be resolved quickly, allowing her to move on and search for another boat. Left with no other concerns, she was left to ponder the intricacies of her relationship with Steve and question whether it existed, as this would determine her future course of action after dealing with the insurance company.

She was so in love with him that she would happily uproot her life and move to Baltimore if he requested, even though he clearly needed to learn how to communicate with a woman when he was upset. That made her smile. The poor man had looked horrified when he'd realized his mistake. There was some hope for him after all.

Chapter Twenty-Three

ANTICIPATING HIS FRIENDS' arrival at Duke's, Romeo carefully selected a strategic spot and ordered three frosty beers for the table. Who cared how early it was? Cleaning up from an explosion deserved beer.

His chosen location in the bar allowed him to maintain a watchful eye on Daisy Mae, ensuring she remained within his line of sight while offering a clear view of the entrance and kitchen door.

"Let me guess," Grits sighed as he sat, "you earned your nickname again."

Casper chuckled as he sat.

"Fuck ya, both." Steve couldn't care less if they knew he had fucked up with Daisy Mae. It was how she felt about it that mattered. Without taking his eyes off his woman, he asked his brethren, "Status?"

Romeo caught snippets of his friend's words, "The twins—" before Daisy Mae's laughter enveloped his ears. At that moment, he felt relief seeing her joy despite the weight of the morning's events.

"Earth to Romeo." Grits snapped his fingers in front of Romeo's face, bringing him back to the table and its occupants.

"*Mais, oui.* Go ahead."

"Boy, your accent and wording have gone south with your brains. Get your mind off the girl in that way and think like a damn agent. Her life depends upon it."

Grit's final words had a substantial impact on Romeo. He straightened his posture and cleared his mind from the previous evening. "*Merde.* I be focused."

"On what?" Casper asked as he tossed some peanuts in his mouth.

"Don't be provoking me, Casper," Romeo said, prepared to strike whoever was involved in what happened to Daisy Mae, whether it was their fault or not. "Go ahead, Grits."

"Well," Grits said as he glanced around their table, "you've got a mess on your hands."

Romeo wanted to growl. Instead, he sipped his beer and said, "That's why ya be here."

"The twins aren't copping to having stolen the map. They point the finger at Mario for all that has gone wrong. Mario points the finger at the twins and even Daisy Mae. We plan to speak with Antionne next and see what the big-time treasure hunter says. He may have nothing to do with this."

"In other words, ya haven't learned shit." Romeo hoped his disappointment didn't show in his voice because he knew his teammates were working hard on the case. He couldn't accept failure on this problem. Someone blew up her boat. She could have been on it. That was what got to him the most. Whoever decided to destroy her livelihood could have easily taken her life. He wouldn't settle for anything other than catching the villain.

"I wouldn't say that," Grits said as he raised a hand to order another round for them.

"I'm good." Romeo only wanted the news. "Tell me what ya learned." And why the hell hadn't Grits and Casper led with that? He'd discuss that with them at another time, but his focus now had to be on Daisy Mae's safety.

Grits took a long draw of beer and then set the glass down. "It appears that everyone in town knows the twins have a treasure map."

"*Merde.*"

"Exactly. That means our suspect pool is larger than expected."

"Can ya handle it, or should we call in more of da boys?"

Grits and Casper looked at each other for a minute, then Casper shrugged. Grits spoke for the two. "We can handle the groundwork. But I think you need extra security for Daisy Mae."

Romeo felt like he'd been thrown in the bayou at the deep end with weights around his ankles and gators on the prowl. "What the fuck? I can guard her."

"As your team leader, I'm telling you that you can't." Grits firmly set to his features, telling Romeo he'd play the team leader card as long as needed to get his way. As only second in command, Romeo was to obey. He could argue, but in the end, if Grits felt he was right, that was the way the team rolled.

But this wasn't an HIS-sanctioned op. This was his problem that his friends were helping him with. Wasn't it? He didn't want someone watching over Daisy Mae, while he got pulled away. He would be with her twenty-four-seven.

"I be with her always, so we no need help."

"What about when you're sleeping?" Casper asked.

Again, he made sense when he spoke. Someone to watch over them when they slept would be nice, but would Daisy Mae feel comfortable sleeping with him while someone watched over them? Hell, Daisy Mae wouldn't want someone else watching over her period.

Romeo sipped his beer and watched Daisy Mae over the mug's rim. After he set the glass down, he sighed in resignation. His teammates were right. "She won't go for it."

"Well, buddy," Grits said, "it's your job to convince her. Until we get someone in place, Casper will be your backup. I can handle the questioning alone."

So, they'd already had a plan whether he agreed or not. *Merde.* When had he lost control of things? This was his op if they wanted to call it that. Romeo stared at Casper. "How ghostly can ya be?"

"She won't even notice I'm around," his teammate confidently said.

Romeo looked at his half-empty mug and wiped at the water sliding down the side. Maybe he could avoid telling her, and things could continue normally. What the hell was typical? She'd been in trouble since he'd been home. He shuddered at the thought of it all. His gut twisted thinking about the bullets flying at her and then the explosion. What was next?

He nodded. "*Mais oui.* Call in da boys. Only what ya need, and be discreet." He turned from Grits to Casper. "Ya had best be as transparent as a ghost. If she sees ya, she might just shoot ya."

Casper chuckled. The asshole chuckled. He didn't realize Romeo was serious. Daisy Mae would not tolerate her space being invaded any more than it had already been. Hell, would she allow him back into that space after he'd gone and stuck his large ass foot in his mouth?

"Who ya want to call in?" Romeo asked Grits, ignoring Casper altogether.

"I'm thinking Kate and Rylee. You could use women here for Daisy Mae."

If Rylee came, Devon would come, meaning the Hamilton brothers might expect to get paid for their work. He couldn't blame them but didn't relish wiping out his savings. If it made Daisy Mae comfortable and safe, he'd do whatever it took. It was a good thing Jesse was on a mission, or he'd show, and Romeo wouldn't know how he'd manage to regain control.

"Ya know dat means Devon, right? Which means da big boss might have something to say about how we be using our time off."

"Let me worry about the big boss," Grits said. "You worry about returning to Daisy Mae's good graces and prep her for the whirlwind that is Rylee."

That was all he needed—two head-strong, gun-toting, take-no-prisoners women. His head hurt already.

Chapter Twenty-Four

DAISY MAE WAS furious as Sheriff's Deputy Alice Fournier refused to assist her in bringing Mario Xenos to justice, citing "legal search," "probable cause," and "warrant" as reasons. Daisy Mae didn't care about those things.

Single-minded in her determination, Daisy Mae understood the urgency of the situation. They had to act quickly to search Mario's boat and home. If they didn't, they risked losing vital evidence needed to prove that he was responsible for planting the bomb that destroyed her boat.

"What be the matter?" Steve asked her from the driver's side of her truck. She couldn't fathom why she had agreed to let him drive her home. She was resolute that he wouldn't be staying. He would simply have to journey back to where he belonged on foot.

She crossed her arms like a sullen child and looked out the side window. "Not a thing."

"Come on, Rocket. Ya be pouting worse than when ya could no stay the night at my house when ya be six."

Great. She found herself revisiting a profoundly embarrassing moment from her past. Perplexed by her parents' refusal to let her spend the night at her friend's house, she reflected on how, at that time, she lacked an understanding of the distinctions between boys and girls despite having two older brothers. All she knew was that she was determined to marry Steve and yearned to be by his side constantly.

"Alice. She be refusing to search Mario's *bateau* for evidence." There, she'd said it.

Steve turned into her tiny home's driveway. "She be right. Besides, you not know if it be him or someone else."

Grabbing the door handle, she turned to him. "I know it be him. Now, go home."

Steve chuckled. "When ya gonna get it, Rocket? Where ya go, I go."

"Ya, no, stay here, Steve." He had to throw a wrench into her plans, but what a good night they could have if she wanted him to stay. She did not, though. *Merde.* How could she possibly sneak out and search Mario's boat if he stayed? This dilemma plagued her, the excitement of an undercover search conflicting with her desire for him to spend the night between the sheets with her.

Ignoring her, he exited the truck and stepped toward her home, not the road back to town. *Mais*, he could stay the night. She'd have to find a way to search anyway. Just because he stayed the night didn't mean she couldn't sneak out. But how with his super-agent-hearing?

She stood there as she slammed her truck door, watching him turn and push the lock button on the key fob. After the reassuring beep, she stepped toward him and her welcoming home. After the break-in, she hurriedly straightened up the place, but it still looked unsuitable for visitors. Given the chance, she would have liked to clean the place thoroughly.

Daisy Mae unlocked her front door and stepped into her home. She stopped and couldn't believe it. It had been tossed again. What the ever-loving-hell?

Steve stepped inside, drew his weapon, and pushed her behind him. *Merde*. When would he learn?

"Stay here, Rocket."

She would do no such thing. Instead, she followed him from the living room to each of the two bedrooms, the kitchen, and the bathrooms—nothing but destruction.

"Why?" she wondered out loud.

Steve holstered his weapon and reached out, pulling her into his arms.

Daisy Mae tensed up initially but then gradually eased into the comforting embrace. Despite her efforts, she ultimately succumbed to an overwhelming flood of tears. Why would someone do this to her? She had always been kind to everyone. The thought of Mario crossed her mind. Well, almost everyone. But to toss her place twice? Who would go to such lengths? Were they acting out of pettiness or searching for something they hadn't found and hoped she had hidden after the first ransacking of her office?

Mario had been absent after she went to Duke's with Alice. He could have done this. She stiffened and pulled from Steve's embrace. "Mario, he do this."

"How can ya be knowing dat?" Steve asked. "He be wit us most of the day cleaning up the dock."

"Yeah, but he be missing when we go inside." She strode toward the kitchen, ensuring no open food might spoil. She would start cleaning in this room.

Steve followed her. "Surely he go home to shower. We be grimy and sooty."

Mais oui. She needed a shower. They both smelled like a fire, but her home had to be cleaned.

Touching her shoulder, Steve said. "Daisy Mae, ya shower first, and I'll start to clean."

Daisy Mae hesitated.

"Go on. I'll start here. When ya be done, I'll shower, and ya can clean."

Seeing the wisdom in his words and her need for some deep thought that could only happen in the shower or a bath, she consented. "*Merci.*"

As she left Steve to deal with the mess, she went to the bedroom and found a fresh set of clothes. Stepping into the shower once it was hot and steamy, she stood still under the comforting spray, allowing the warm water to cascade over her, melting away the day's stress. She reached for the soap bar, ready to wash away the remnants of a long day.

As she washed the soot from her face, she pondered her dilemma. She needed someone to be a friend to her and search Mario's boat and home with her or for her. She couldn't ask her friends since it was illegal, and she'd never ask them to do something that could put them in jail.

She stopped and rinsed her face. Would Alice put her in jail if she caught her snooping? Probably not, but Alice wasn't the only deputy. Thank goodness they weren't large enough for their own police department and depended upon the overstretched sheriff's department for assistance. She could be in and out before anyone knew she'd been there.

But how was she to get past Steve?

The inky black color slowly faded as she lathered her hair with shampoo, revealing her tangled thoughts. At that moment, an idea struck her—a daring and potentially risky one if not executed perfectly. Nevertheless, it ignited a spark of excitement within her.

It was enough. She finished bathing until her skin gleamed, then exited the shower to moisturize and dress. She had a plan to implement to prove Mario was behind this mess and get it over with.

Steve would not be the wiser to her plans. Nor would he be able to stop her.

Chapter Twenty-Five

DISCONNECTING HIS CALL to Brad, Romeo had never seen a pair of shorts and a tank top look so good on a woman as they did on Daisy Mae. He loved her with her hair in her iconic ball cap. Yet, as he saw her now, with her hair down, wet and unadorned, an overpowering urge swept over him to take her by the hand and whisk her away to the bedroom…or floor…or wall…. He wasn't picky with her.

Daisy Mae's eyes flashed angrily as she placed her hands on her hips. "Did I just hear ya say more people be coming?" she demanded, her tone laced with frustration.

Pulled back from a haze of desire, Romeo gave a confirming nod. After mentally regathering himself, he spoke, "*Oui*. Two of me teammates will arrive soon."

Daisy Mae stamped her foot. "*Non! Non! Non!* This be too much."

"Rocket, ya need the protection, and I be having to sleep sometime." He took a step forward and smiled. "Unless ya decided I be staying after all."

She narrowed her eyes at him. "Ya know ya get to stay."

When Daisy Mae admitted her agreement, it felt like a significant win for him. He knew he would stay, but her explicit confirmation made everything smoother.

"After all that be happening, ya must agree someone be out to hurt ya. Ya need protection until we resolve dis thing."

Daisy Mae's demeanor deflated before his very eyes. She slowly reached back and lowered herself onto a barstool as if she could no longer bear to stand. Softly and barely audible, she said, "I no want to be in danger."

He moved forward to hold her and then smelled himself. He smelled like smoke, and she'd just showered. So, he kept his distance, not wanting to taint the pleasant smell of whatever she'd lathered on her silky skin. "No one be wanting dat. But, we be here to help. It be what I do for a living. Let us help."

If she were to refuse, he couldn't anticipate his next move. He would, without a doubt, stay put. The boys would continue their investigation, but the women wouldn't be effective as bodyguards if Daisy Mae didn't permit them to be near her.

She finally looked up at him. "Who be coming and what they be doing?"

He wanted to fist-pump his celebration. "Two gals to be around ya all the time. One works while the other sleeps. Ya will like dem."

"Even when I go to da bathroom?"

He shook his head. "They no watch, but they check it out for safety."

"Dat be excessive, Steve."

"*Non*. It be called 'Protection 101.'" Which also stated not to get involved with your client, but he could care less about that part of the rule. Surrounded by the company of Kate and Rylee, he would feel free from the pressures of constant threats, allowing him to refocus his attention on Daisy Mae. He hoped that in doing so, he could ultimately convince her to abandon her current situation and accompany him back to Baltimore. He would work to purchase a new boat for her, allowing her to offer charters along the Thames. He was sure she'd love it.

Daisy Mae remained quiet for a long moment, making him wonder if she would decide against the extra protection.

So she couldn't say no right away, he said, "Listen, the kitchen be clean, and I need a shower. How 'bout we finish dis conversation after dat?"

She nodded silently as he walked past her, trying to maintain a safe distance. However, a moment later, he hesitated, took a step back, and tenderly kissed her on the cheek. "It all be okay, Rocket."

Romeo walked outside to retrieve his bag from the truck. His phone rang as he pressed the key fob to unlock it. *Devon*. He was confident that the man would reach out to him at some point, especially since Romeo had recently requested his wife for a mission.

Balancing the phone between his shoulder and cheek, he deftly reached for the truck door and swung it open. "Dev, what be up?"

"Is she walking into serious trouble?"

Romeo couldn't help but stifle a laugh. Devon constantly fretted about Rylee whenever she embarked on an operation, but little did Devon know that Rylee was more formidable than he was. She possessed extensive FBI training and could manage herself in any situation. Additionally, she would be furious if she found out that Devon had been making these calls to team members who had specifically requested her presence for an operation.

"*Non, chèr.* Besides, we be here to back her up."

"This had best be because you've fallen in love with the client and need female protection for her 24/7. Otherwise—"

Romeo must've made a noise that stopped Devon.

"You have fallen for her. Haven't you?"

With a heavy sigh, he admitted, "Many years ago."

"Well, we'll take care of her. I'm coming also. Anything I need to know ahead of time?"

He considered what they needed to know and referred him to his teammate. "Grits be the man to speak with. He be doing the investigation and needs more help. I be fine." That wasn't true, but Grits would fill him in on everything, so why muddy up the waters with more fingers in the pot?

"All right. We can't get there until tomorrow afternoon, so hang tight."

"*Merci, chèr.*" After finishing their call, Romeo swiftly retrieved his bag from the truck. Once he securely closed and locked the vehicle, he walked back toward Daisy Mae's home, eager for a shower. He considered leaving the windows down on the truck to help with the odor, but the forecast called for light showers in the early morning hours. They'd deal with it tomorrow.

He came to a halt as he entered the room. Daisy Mae was meticulously tidying up the living room, focused on the discarded items she had placed in the trash bag. She didn't glance up when he walked in. He noticed tears trickling down her cheeks. She kept her head down, unwilling to let him see her cry. He understood her need for privacy and quietly went to the guest bathroom.

As he entered the bathroom, he unceremoniously dropped his bag onto the floor and wearily leaned on the sink. Envisioning her tear-streaked face, he longed to envelop her in a reassuring embrace, to offer solace and assure her that everything would eventually fall into place. However, he couldn't promise that until they found out who was behind the explosion that destroyed her boat. No matter what he told her, things were serious. Whoever was responsible wasn't playing. They meant business.

He wished he'd had the full force of HIS behind them right now, but the teams were disbursed elsewhere. Plus, there was no real need except for his peace of mind. The six of them—Grits, Casper, Rylee, Kate, Devon, and him—should be enough to protect one woman.

Then, he considered her brothers. They'd also had their home ransacked. But they hadn't been shot at or had their boat blown to bits. Would they want protection? Doubtful, but he'd have to check. They were her brothers, and he knew Daisy Mae loved them no matter how much they fought.

Sighing, he turned on the shower and began to undress. Those clothes were destined for the trash as he doubted the smell of smoke would ever leave the fabric.

As he stood in the warm spray of the shower, he watched intently as the inky black water swirled down the drain, mesmerized by the gradual transition to clarity. He could feel the soothing lather of the soap as it worked its way across his skin, carrying away the day's residue and leaving him refreshed and clean. He longed to summon the courage to invite her to relocate to Baltimore with him, but he couldn't shake off the uncertainty of how she would react. Although they hadn't been officially together for an extended period, it was increasingly clear that they had both harbored feelings for each other for quite some time. Would it be enough? It would be for him, but he would ask her to leave everything behind. Was that fair?

It may be time for him to leave HIS and settle in his hometown.

Chapter Twenty-Six

AS DAISY MAE gazed at the wreckage in her living room, a pang of despair welled, but she pushed it aside. She had always believed that dwelling on negative emotions was an obstacle to progress. With a deep breath, she resolved to tackle the chaos and continue her life. Yet, tears streamed down her face, and she was sure Steve had noticed them as he walked past.

Wiping the tears from her eyes, she strengthened her determination to solve the mystery and restore balance to her life. *Mario.*

Excited and determined, she eagerly anticipated the opportunity to search Mario's boat that night because Steve and his friends had refused to assist her. They embraced the virtues of honor, law, justice, and other similar ideals. Their boat hadn't been the one that exploded, and their homes hadn't been ransacked not once but twice. Frustrated and determined, she had reached her limit and decided to gather evidence and build a case against Mario, if necessary, to end his actions.

By the time Steve came out of the shower, she had tidied up the living room and her bedroom. Despite its imperfections, her home was a sanctuary she cherished dearly. While material possessions could be destroyed, her unwavering love for her home remained indestructible.

Feeling embarrassed after shedding tears earlier, Daisy Mae could not meet Steve's gaze. Instead, she lowered her head and made her way to the kitchen. "I be making us some dinner."

"I be glad to help."

"*Non!*" She realized she'd already screamed it and softened her reply. "*Non*. I'll cook. Ya relax. Ya worked hard today." He had bravely worked to halt the spread of the fire and rescued her remaining possessions from the water. He had to be exhausted.

"So did ya," he said from the doorway to the kitchen.

As she turned, her eyes locked with his, and a surge of heat coursed through her veins at the mere sight of him. He dressed entirely in black, sporting a fresh black ball cap. She assumed it was new, considering it didn't carry the faint scent of smoke. Did he bring a new one on every trip? How odd and anal.

"I be fine. Now, go. Talk to the people ya need to talk to to get some answers. I will cook." She lightly pushed him to get him out of the kitchen.

At first, she thought he'd catch her hands, but he let her remove him from the room.

"I do need to catch up with Grits. Are ya sure it be okay?"

"*Oui.*" She turned and opened the small pantry, hoping something was left to cook. All her meat and seafood had been spoiled, so packaged food it was. She looked over her scant options and decided on a meatless jambalaya, peas she'd canned, and homemade biscuits. It wasn't gourmet, but it would fill their gullets.

The first thing she did was boil some water to make tea. She longed for a tall, chilled glass of iced tea to soothe her parched throat. Despite drinking water all day to stay hydrated, nothing could match the revitalizing taste of sweet, iced tea.

Next, she began working on dinner. It took just over half an hour to prepare everything, but she had managed to crush the powder for Steve's drink. Despite feeling guilty, she knew she had no choice but to search the boat tonight. With more people arriving tomorrow, she couldn't wait, no matter how she felt.

"Dinner be ready," she shouted to Steve, who had been on the phone nearly the entire time she'd been grinding and cooking.

"Hmm. Smells good."

Daisy Mae was startled as she felt someone sneak up on her. She couldn't believe he had approached her so silently. She hoped he hadn't seen her grinding the sleeping powder with the surviving mortar and pestle.

"Grab ya a plate and bring it to the table." She fixed herself a plate and grabbed water instead of iced tea. She'd had some before she added the sleeping powder to it for Steve. She hoped it was just enough, not too much. She didn't want to harm him, only make him sleep so she could sneak away.

"Interesting mix of things for dinner, but good," Steve said, grabbing a mouthful of biscuits. Her brothers had always said she made the best biscuits in the family.

She smiled and served him more iced tea. By the end of dinner, he was yawning.

Steve pushed his chair from the table and stretched. "Rocket, that be the best meal me had today."

Beaming, she picked up their plates and headed to the kitchen.

"Ya cooked, I clean," he said behind her.

"*Non.* Ya be more tired than me. Go lie down, and I be right there."

He yawned again, and she inwardly smiled. *Not long now.* "Go, Steve. I already cleaned all but our plates."

"Okay. If ya be sure."

Daisy Mae nodded. "I be there in a minute. I need to wash these real fast-like." A dishwasher was on her list of kitchen upgrades, but she had become skilled at handwashing quickly.

She carefully scrubbed each dish, letting the warm water and soapy suds soothe her thoughts. After meticulously wiping down the table and counters, she straightened the kitchen towels, purposely taking her time. Eventually, she leisurely made her way to the bedroom, savoring each step as a moment of respite in her busy day.

As she arrived in her bedroom, she smiled at a snoring Steve, still dressed, on the covers of her bed. "Steve?" she called to confirm he was good and out cold.

When he didn't answer, grunt, or move, she knew this was her chance. Daisy Mae quickly rushed to her ornate wooden dresser, her hands skimming over the smooth surface in search of the perfectly coordinated outfit. She carefully chose a sleek pair of black shorts and a matching black tank top from the neatly folded clothes. A few moments later, she stepped over to her closet, where an array of hats awaited her. After a brief perusal, she discovered a predominantly black hat with striking white lettering, which she knew would complement her outfit flawlessly for the occasion. She almost snorted out loud for ensuring she matched for this outing.

She felt ready when she donned her short, black combat boots with black socks. At least, she'd dressed the part. Once again, when she called for Steve, she was relieved when he appeared out for the count. She didn't know how long she had, but she had to make the most of each moment.

Grabbing the keys to the truck from by the front door, she quietly snuck from the house. She planned to thoroughly search Mario's boat tonight, knowing she wouldn't have any time to herself after the other agents arrived.

As Daisy Mae carefully steered the truck near the dock, she couldn't help but notice the bustling activity at Duke's. Clearly, the business was thriving, with customers coming and going steadily. She hoped no one saw her sneaking around the boats.

Daisy Mae's heart pounded in her chest as uncertainty clouded her thoughts. However, her emotions quickly shifted when she realized the vacant space where *Seas the Day* had been anchored. Anger surged within her once more.

As she exited the truck, she tugged her cap down low and cautiously glanced around, scanning the empty dock to ensure no one was present. Given that no one resided on their boats, it seemed unlikely that any owners would be nearby.

Using the flashlight from her phone, she made her way to Mario's boat, *Paroles du village*. She always thought "Talk of the Town" was a silly name for a boat, but clients loved it.

With her heart pounding so loudly that she couldn't hear anything but its relentless beat, she leaped onto the bow of Mario's boat. She stood motionless for a moment, scanning her surroundings for any lingering patrons from the bar. Not a soul was in sight, confirming that she had evaded any potential encounters.

As Daisy Mae approached the cockpit and stepped inside, she knew she was running out of time. Steve could wake up soon and realize that she was gone. Once he did, he would send all the men out to look for her, and more than just the women would arrive tomorrow.

If only she knew what evidence she needed to show them that it was Mario.

Before she could even take a single step toward her search, a strong hand suddenly covered her mouth from behind, sending a jolt of fear through her body.

Chapter Twenty-Seven

"SHH," CAME A whispered voice in Daisy Mae's ear, unfamiliar to her.

As she braced to retaliate, she suddenly caught a sound from above. A faint noise indicated that someone was present on the deck. Two threats were before her, creating a palpable sense of unease. The overwhelming odds were stacked against her, but she was determined to muster every ounce of strength and resourcefulness to break free from the clutches of the one restraining her and the other ominously positioned on the deck.

The voice whispered again in her ear, a soft, cautionary sound. This time, she recognized it immediately. Ash's voice echoed in the air, making her wonder if he had followed her. She quickly contemplated if this meant Steve was on deck but dismissed the possibility. She reasoned that Ash wouldn't silence her from a friend.

As the steps from above approached the stairway, Ash guided them into the lavatory, which was a tight space. She was pressed against him, and unlike Steve, it wasn't as comfortable.

Daisy Mae interpreted a string of French words that flew through the air. *Mario.* As he combed through the lower deck of his boat, Daisy Mae couldn't shake off the unsettling thought that someone else might have maliciously planted explosives on her boat instead unless Mario expected a retaliatory strike from her and her friends.

If Mario wasn't the one, then who could it be? She was confident it couldn't be the treasure hunter, as she didn't possess the map—her brothers did. Then again, their place had also been ransacked.

The beads of sweat trickled down her back, and her heart raced with anxiety. She couldn't shake the fear that Mario would soon inspect the small lavatory where she and Ash had taken cover. She was consumed with worry about what would happen if he found them. Would he jump to the conclusion that she was the one responsible for planting the explosives?

As Mario meticulously checked the boat, his frustrated mutterings in a rapid string of incomprehensible French words indicated his inebriation. His speech was slurred, making it evident that he had been drinking.

As Daisy Mae slowly realized that Casper's hand was still covering her mouth, she cautiously raised her hand and carefully removed his. As she did so, her elbow inadvertently knocked against the wall with a soft thud, sending a jolt of dread through her. Her heart raced, worried that the noise may have alerted Mario to their presence.

She stood frozen in paralyzing fear, a sick feeling in her stomach, anticipating the creak of the door opening and the inevitable moment of being caught snooping. However, to her immense relief, that moment never came.

The next sound that reached her ears was initially unfamiliar, but despite this, she made the conscious decision to remain still.

Then Ash—no, he'd earned his nickname Casper by sneaking up on her—murmured, "Well, hell." He leaned close to her ear, his breath warm against her skin, and softly commanded, "Stay quiet." She desperately clutched at his arm as he reached for the doorknob, but he callously shook her off. At that moment, she couldn't help but wonder what kind of bodyguard he was about to jeopardize their safety like this.

Casper whispered, "He's asleep," as he slowly turned the doorknob and peered out, checking both directions to ensure it was safe. After confirming that the coast was clear, he carefully emerged from their hiding spot and extended his hand to help her out as well.

She couldn't believe it. As she entered the room, she saw Mario lying face down on his bed, fast asleep and snoring loudly. She shook her head, amazed at his ability to sleep through anything. She had come perilously close to being discovered while searching through his boat. She felt immense relief from Casper's unexpected intervention. Nevertheless, she resolved to have a serious conversation with him once it was safe to do so regarding his decision to tail her.

Daisy Mae cautiously halted her search, realizing the danger of continuing further. She quietly trailed behind Casper, following his soft footsteps up the ladder and onto the deck. As they reached the pier, they quickened their pace, their footsteps echoing in the stillness of the night.

After a while, Daisy felt they had put enough distance between themselves and any potential eavesdroppers. She came to a stop, preparing herself to confront Casper finally.

"Why do ya follow me?" she hurled at him, anger bleeding into every syllable.

Casper shifted his weight back onto his heels and arched his eyebrows, giving off an air of familiarity with being challenged by a woman. "Because you needed it," he responded confidently.

She truly needed it, although he had no idea at the time. Even as Mario frantically searched his boat, she couldn't shake the feeling in her bones that it was him. As she needed to search his home, the opportune moment had arrived: he was inebriated and passed out on his boat. How could she possibly rid herself of Casper? Alternatively, was there a way she could persuade him to accompany her on the search?

"What have you done to Romeo? He would never have permitted you to depart unaccompanied."

She likely couldn't count on his help when it came to searching Mario's home, so she contemplated how she could remove him from the situation. With Steve and Mario both sleeping blissfully, now was the perfect time. She had to try to convince Casper of that point.

"He just sleeps." She silently prayed that he was still deep in slumber. If he were to awaken and find her absent, she knew there would be a storm of fury to face.

"Uh-huh. Did you hit him on the head or something? Is he hurt?"

"*Non.*" She had done the "or something" but wouldn't admit it. "Ya can go now. I be fine. I be going to visit me *frères* at the bar."

"Right, and I'm the tooth fairy."

"I no see wings," she teased.

Casper narrowed his eyes. "You're going to Mario's house now, right?"

"*Non!*" she nearly shouted, giving herself away.

"That's it. We're heading back," Casper directed.

"I no go, and ya can't make me," she said. "Tonight be the only night I can search. Since ya bunch of wusses won't do it, I must."

"Wusses? Are you kidding? We won't do it because it breaks the law, Daisy Mae."

"Well, I no care about dat. I will prove Mario blew up me *bateau*."

"So," Casper said, narrowing his eyes, "you won't go home now?"

Daisy Mae shook her head. "I be safe with Mario sleeping. Don't ya get it? He be the one."

Casper let out a heavy sigh and addressed Daisy Mae, "We have our doubts about him. After seeing his behavior tonight, I'm even less inclined to believe he's the one who blew up your boat."

Daisy Mae was seething with frustration, her urge to throw a fit and stomp her foot almost overwhelming. Why couldn't they see the truth? She had a history with Mario, but they chose not to believe her. It was clear to her that Mario was trying to push her out of the picture so that his charter could dominate the bayou without any competition.

"I no believe you. I know it be him."

Casper shrugged. "It doesn't matter what you believe now. What matters is we get you home and check on Romeo. Now, let's go."

She planted her hands firmly on her hips and defiantly held her ground, shaking her head. "*Non*," she exclaimed. Determined not to return home empty-handed, she would go to Mario's house to thoroughly search for evidence.

Casper arched a brow. "Is that right? Okay, we do it the hard way."

In a whirlwind of confusion, Daisy Mae suddenly found herself effortlessly lifted over Casper's shoulder. As she came to terms with this unexpected turn of events, she gazed down at his broad, T-shirt-covered back.

She pounded on his back, anger flooding her veins. "Put me down," she exclaimed.

"Not happening. You're going home like a good little girl, and we're checking on my friend."

"Put me down, Casper."

"Looks like you finally got my name right."

Daisy Mae rolled her eyes in frustration, wondering who cared about his name. All she wanted was to be set down, and she wanted it to happen immediately.

He paid her no attention as he briskly walked along the pier. Daisy Mae resigned herself to the realization that she would be lifted and carried to her vehicle, feeling like a wayward child.

It finally dawned on her to ask, "How ya know where I be?"

"Didn't Romeo tell you? I'm your bodyguard while he sleeps. I've been watching your place and saw you sneak out."

When she got home, Steve would have a lot to answer for. She was confident that he wouldn't be pleased when he discovered that she had drugged him to search Mario's boat.

She wondered if her actions would drive him away. Although she didn't seek protection, she longed for Steve to stand by her. Did she make a major mistake tonight?

Maybe her tooth fairy would carry her to a world where things were perfect.

Chapter Twenty-Eight

ROMEO AWOKE SLOWLY, feeling groggy and disoriented. He rolled over in bed, struggling to open his heavy eyelids. Surprised by how deeply he had slept, he couldn't shake off the sensation of drowsiness that clung to him.

He quickly became aware that something was not quite right. He had never experienced such a deep slumber during an assignment before. His eyes popped open. *Daisy Mae!* Even without calling her, he knew that he was by himself.

He found himself waking up alone in a confused state. Realizing that he was fully clothed and not under the covers as he had expected, he suspected that she must have drugged him. *The tea.* She hadn't consumed any of it, and it had a bitter taste that he'd refrained from mentioning. How had he missed it?

As he eased himself off the bed, he heard the front door creak swinging open. Processing the situation, conflicting emotions swirled in his mind. On one hand, he was consumed by anger at her for drugging him and putting herself at risk by leaving. On the other hand, he felt relieved that she had returned unharmed.

As he hastily approached the bedroom door, it swung open, revealing Casper. Dressed entirely in black, his concerned expression was visible in the dimly lit room.

"Thank ya," Romeo said before Casper could speak.

The agent nodded, turned, and walked back into the living room.

As Romeo stood there, bracing himself for the impending confrontation, he couldn't shake off his uncertainty about handling the situation. The clenching knots in his gut wouldn't allow him to forget the fact that she had not only drugged him but also made the reckless decision to venture off alone, fully aware of the potential danger to her safety.

As he made his way into the living room, he spotted Daisy Mae settled in an armchair, her arms tightly crossed, shooting an evil glare in Casper's direction. The agent must've intervened just in time to prevent her from causing trouble.

Romeo glanced around and noticed Daisy Mae abruptly standing up from her seat. Rather than confronting him about assigning Casper to watch over her, she handled the situation differently, completely throwing him off.

She rushed to him. "I be so sorry, Steve. Ya be okay?"

He peered at her through narrowed eyes, trying to discern the meaning behind her words. Unsure of what she was trying to convey, he hesitated momentarily before giving a simple nod. Was she genuinely showing concern or simply using flattery to gain his support in the impending debate about her protection detail?

Her worry was palpable as she wrung her hands, emphasizing her distress. "I didn't mean to do it, but ya left me no choice," she confessed with a quiver in her voice.

He knew that wasn't the least bit true, but he only raised an eyebrow in response. "Really now?"

"It be Mario, and it feels like no one listens to me. Can't ya see? I had to prove it all by myself." She turned to Casper and pointed a finger accusingly. "And den he stopped me."

"I saved your ass," Casper replied firmly as he wearily dropped onto the couch and ran a hand over his tired face. "You're extremely fortunate that I intervened before Mario had a chance to confront you."

She put her hands on her hips. "I coulda handled myself."

Romeo bellowed, "Enough!" His voice was unexpectedly loud, but the frustration just poured out of him. He looked at Daisy Mae. "Sit," he directed.

Shock etched on Daisy Mae's face, she hurried to claim the empty armchair.

Casper attempted to leave, but Romeo halted him. "Stay," Romeo insisted, and Casper acquiesced with a nod.

"What the hell happened tonight?"

As Daisy Mae started to speak, Romeo interrupted her abruptly. "Ya already admitted to drugging me and leaving. I want to hear from Casper," he demanded.

Daisy Mae huffed in frustration and crossed her arms, displaying a petulant and childish demeanor.

Casper began, "I watched the house and saw her sneak out. Unsure of what was happening, I followed her."

"And ya had no concern for me? That she'd been able to leave alone?"

The agent casually nonchalantly lifted his shoulders. "I considered it more crucial to keep tabs on her, as I was certain she had no intention of causing you any harm."

As Romeo turned over those profound words in his mind, he couldn't help but acknowledge their undeniable truth. It also struck him that the course of action described was exactly what he would have chosen in that situation.

"Anyhow, she went to Mario's boat."

"And ya just let her?" Romeo asked.

"Well, yeah. I wanted to see what she was up to."

Romeo heaved a heavy sigh as he contemplated the peril Daisy Mae could have faced if someone had planted explosives on Mario's boat. Despite the looming danger, he left it and said, "Go on."

"After arriving at the pier, I saw Mario leaving the bar, so I confronted Daisy Mae."

"Scared the bejesus out of me was more like it," she huffed.

"We hid. Mario passed out. We left. And here we are."

Romeo suddenly realized that Casper had left out a few details, but after grasping the situation's essence, he decided to press on.

"Why?" he asked Daisy Mae. "I told ya we be investigating. Ya no need to do it."

"'Cause no one listens to me. It be Mario."

Romeo's voice reverberated through the room as he emphatically stated, "*Non*, it's not. We cleared Mario. He not be the threat we're here to find."

Daisy Mae's eyes widened with fervor as she leaped up from her chair, her voice filled with certainty as she declared, "Yes, he be! I know it!"

Romeo's gaze was unwavering as he pointed to the chair. "Sit."

After Daisy Mae took her seat, Romeo crossed his arms over his chest and gestured toward Casper, indicating that he should be the one to speak. "Tell her," Romeo urged, his eyes fixed on Casper, awaiting his response.

Casper cleared his throat and addressed the situation with precision. "Firstly, Mario has solid alibis for the time when your house was ransacked. Secondly, we thoroughly searched his place and found no trace of any explosives. Lastly, it's evident that trouble seems to be following both you and your brothers, which indicates the culprits' interest isn't specifically focused on you."

"Ya searched his place and didn't tell me?" Daisy Mae asked, her voice filled with hurt and disbelief.

Romeo nodded solemnly. "I planned to sit down with ya after dinner and reveal everything."

Daisy Mae winced. She'd been the one to ruin that plan. "Then who it be?"

Romeo took a seat in the open armchair. "We no be sure. Yet. But we have eliminated Mario. That be a step in the right direction."

Casper chimed in. "We're still investigating the treasure hunter and other potentials."

Cocking her head in question, Daisy Mae asked, "What other potentials?"

Romeo knew they would need to disclose it at some juncture. With that in mind, the present moment seemed as opportune as any for the revelation. "Local ones."

Daisy Mae shook her head. "No one local would blow up me *bateau*."

"Are ya willing to bet ya life on that?" Romeo asked.

She opened her mouth to say something but closed it. After thinking for a moment, she said, "*Non.*"

Finally, they would have her follow their every command, ensuring she remained under their constant protection, right where she belonged. Romeo's anxiety spiked at the mere thought of something happening to her. He was immensely grateful that Casper had been on duty that evening; otherwise, he might have lost her, which he found utterly unacceptable.

He wished he could whisk her away now and remove her from the danger, but he knew she wouldn't leave her brothers in danger.

"Why do ya not have protection on me frères?"

Casper and Romeo looked at each other. Romeo decided it must be him who spoke. "Because they be part of the 'local ones' we be investigating."

Chapter Twenty-Nine

DAISY MAE WAS utterly shocked by the accusation hurled. The mere thought of anyone suspecting her brothers of being capable of causing such destruction was unbelievable to her. It shook her to the core and left her grappling with disbelief and confusion.

"Me *frères*? They no blow up me *bateau* or shoot at me."

Steve leaned forward and placed his forearms on his thighs. "We no say they did. We think dey stole the map, and dat makes dem suspicious-like."

She had been consumed by the fear that her brothers, whom she had loved, were the ones who had taken the precious map. Despite the evidence pointing in their direction, she struggled to accept the possibility, desperately clinging to the hope that the betrayal had come from elsewhere. It was a painful internal conflict between suspicion and loyalty to her flesh and blood.

"*Non*." She shook her head slowly, her voice barely audible as she struggled to express her disbelief. It was a disbelief that was slipping away quickly. If Steve and his agents were convinced that her brothers had stolen the map, then it was becoming increasingly likely that they had indeed taken it. She realized she might have to accept this unsettling possibility.

"During Grit's interview with Antoine Rousseau, he says dat a newly purchased map is currently missing from his possession." Steve stood up and paced around, causing her anxiety to increase significantly. "We cannot be certain if it be the same map, as ya *frères* are not permitting me to inspect it to confirm."

"So, what be the plan to clear me *frères*?"

Steve stopped pacing and sat. "Well, dey mentioned dey needed help carrying da treasure. So, let's see if dey will allow Grits and Casper along."

Daisy Mae shook her head before Steve even finished the sentence. "*Non*. They never agree. But maybe...." Her voice trailed off as she considered an alternative.

"Maybe what?" Casper asked.

"He might allow me friends to go. Dey have gone before—once. But day have gone. Dey be divers, so me *frères* needed divers for dis fictional treasure, before-like."

Steve sat back. "What friends?"

She smiled at the thought of the women breaking the case when these big, bad men couldn't. "Marie *et* Alice."

Casper and Steve looked at each other and spoke silently because they both nodded.

"As long as Romeo is along, that can work," Casper said. "Do you think your brothers would be dangerous to your friends?"

Shaking her head, Daisy Mae said, "*Non.*" Then it dawned on her. "Dey not be the only one ya be investigating, do dey?"

Casper and Steve stared at each other again, and then Steve cleared his throat and turned to her. "Dere are, ah, other people we be looking into."

"Like who?" She wanted to identify her potential threats, although she didn't believe anyone from her hometown, except Mario, would pose a danger to her.

"It not be important."

She had grown frustrated by the lack of progress in a situation that felt like a living nightmare. She decided to seek assistance from her female friends to help her uncover the identity of the person causing her harm. Alice, in particular, was eager to help, as it aligned with her responsibilities as a sheriff's deputy. She possessed the qualifications of Steve and his companions to take on this challenge.

"*Bien.*"

The men gazed at her with wide-eyed astonishment, taken aback by her apparent acceptance of the situation. At that moment, she felt a sense of resignation—what other choice did she have? Despite her attempts to gain information, they refused to disclose anything of use, except for the damning revelation that her brothers were supposedly involved in thievery.

"*Oui. Bien.*" She stood. "Now. I be ready to sleep. Steve, ya have the spare room. Casper, ya have the couch. Goodnight." Then she made her way to her bedroom and closed the door. After a long, calming exhale, she went to the bed and collapsed onto it, burying her face in the pillow as tears streamed down her cheeks. She'd had about all she could take for one day.

Throughout the night, she was tormented by vivid and terrifying nightmares. In these haunting dreams, she saw the faces of familiar individuals from her community, each one brandishing a weapon and taking aim at her as she tried to go about her ordinary activities, like picking up groceries. The fear and helplessness she experienced in these nightmares were so intense that she woke up drenched in sweat, finding it difficult to shake off the lingering sense of dread.

As the first rays of the early morning sun gently streamed through the window, she realized valuable sleep eluded her. She savored the warmth and felt a sense of determination wash over her. After a refreshing shower, she retired to her thoughts, carefully mulling over her situation. She consciously decided at that moment—she refused to remain a victim. The time had come to shift to the offensive, and with Alice standing by her side, she felt a surge of confidence.

She found solace in knowing Alice would also look out for Marie. However, she couldn't help but wish that Shelly didn't have classes to teach. She knew that Shelly's invaluable contributions would greatly assist in solving the case.

As she tiptoed into the kitchen, she set out to prepare a hearty Cajun breakfast for the men, hoping to coax more information from them. Remembering the old adage that "you catch more flies with honey than with vinegar," she decided that a warm, generous gesture might do the trick.

Only, the men were in her kitchen, looking in the cabinets and refrigerator. "What ya be doing?"

Steve turned and blushed. Actually blushed. "We, uh, be cooking breakfast."

They intruded on her life, but they would not intrude on her love of cooking. "Get out of me kitchen," she demanded.

This was her life. She repeated to herself that she was not a victim. She was taking control of things around her. The men could take a step back and allow the women to resolve the conflicts in her life.

Afterward, she found herself contemplating her next move. Should she invest in a new boat, or should she hope for an invitation from Steve to accompany him to Baltimore?

While taking control of her life and safety was easy, finding the answers to those questions remained elusive.

Chapter Thirty

ROMEO WAS ASTOUNDED by how swiftly Daisy Mae orchestrated another exhilarating treasure hunt, uniting everyone for the adventurous quest. The only obstacle they faced was securing a suitable boat. Due to the unavailability of Daisy Mae's more extensive charter, they resorted to utilizing Marie's relatively smaller vessel. Surprisingly, the vessel generously accommodated all six of them, leaving ample space for the treasure her enthusiastic brothers were adamant about discovering.

Romeo's mission was clear: ascertain if the map in question was the stolen one. Despite his belief in Daisy Mae's brothers, he couldn't ignore the possibility that it would have put Daisy Mae in grave danger if they were the culprits. This concern troubled him deeply, adding a sense of peril to the adventure.

It wasn't too difficult to persuade JP and Pierre to permit Marie and Alice to participate in the hunting expedition. The brothers seemed to be under the impression that the haul would be substantial, necessitating additional assistance transporting the goods.

Moreover, they required a boat, and the sisters were the only ones able to provide the discreetness that the brothers valued.

Marie's eyes sparkled with excitement as the gentle wind tousled her long, flowing hair, sweeping it away from her face. "I be excited," she exclaimed. "It be a minute since we last went on a treasure hunt together. I be missing it."

Romeo experienced a surge of excitement as he considered the upcoming events, but he remained steadfast in his commitment to ensuring the crew's safety. He felt reassured by the fact that Alice was also armed, knowing that he could rely on her support in case the situation went sideways.

Alice cautiously inquired about the elusive map, voicing the question Romeo had hesitated to ask directly. "When we be havin' the opportunity to see dis treasure map?"

JP and Pierre looked at each other and shook their heads. "It be for us to see."

Romeo pondered the situation, realizing that it was evident they didn't want the local authorities to discover something. He was almost sure that they possessed the stolen map from Antionne. The pressing issue was how he could retrieve and return it without the brothers ending up in jail. His thoughts turned to Daisy Mae, knowing she would oppose their incarceration.

"Daisy Mae be knowing the direction," JP said. "She takes us dere."

Those were brave words, considering it wasn't JP or Daisy Mae's boat they were using, but Marie only nodded and allowed Daisy Mae to take the helm. And so, with the wind in their hair and the promise of adventure on the horizon, they set off on another treasure hunt. Keenly aware of their dangers, Romeo vowed to remain by Daisy Mae's side on the boat, ensuring she was always protected.

The brothers' behavior grew increasingly guarded and covert as the island appeared on the horizon. Romeo couldn't help but surmise that they were clandestinely working out the distribution of the anticipated treasure, perhaps pondering how much loot each of them would receive. However, he made a mental note that he had no intention of claiming a share, mainly if the treasure was obtained through illicit means such as a stolen map.

It wasn't long before Daisy Mae steered them within swimming range of their mysterious island. "I be going," Daisy Mae said.

"Ya stay with da *bateau*," JP ordered.

"I be going," Daisy Mae argued, resettling her cap on her head and pulling her hair through the loop on the back.

"Someone has to remain onboard," Marie said. "I'll do it."

"*Non*." JP turned from Marie to Daisy Mae. "We need ya to be ready to move should trouble come. Ya know the bayou."

Having had enough and not wanting to see an argument, Romeo said, "*Merde*. I stay with Daisy Mae in da *bateau*. Y'all go ashore."

He heard Daisy Mae huff beside him, her irritation palpable as the others nodded and began moving. He braced himself for the earful he knew he'd receive later but couldn't help but smile at the thought. He relished the fiery spirit within her, stirring emotions in him that he never knew existed.

As Romeo predicted, once the others had slipped into the water and were out of earshot, she turned to him, her eyes flashing angrily. "How dare ya try to control me actions?" she exclaimed, jabbing her thumb towards her chest. "I be a fully grown woman, in case ya forget."

No, he couldn't forget she was grown. In fact, thinking of her in bed with him made his dick begin to twitch to life. For some reason, it had a mind of its own around her.

Romeo's lips curled into a smile as he slowly approached her, his movements reminiscent of a predator closing in on its prey. "I no forget, Rocket. I never be forgetting," he declared with a determined gleam in his eye.

As his hand rose to caress her cheek, he noticed the swift transformation in her eyes from fiery anger to smoldering desire. His love for her surged at that moment. Though he longed to urge her to open up completely, he knew it wasn't the right time, with the possibility of the team returning soon. This moment had to be just right, and he would ensure it.

With his thumb caressing her soft lips, Romeo asked, "Is it so bad staying on da *bateau* with me?"

As if unable to speak, Daisy Mae held his gaze and shook her head.

Romeo gently brushed his thumb aside as he leaned forward to kiss her. When their lips finally met, an explosion of fireworks seemed to sear through his entire being, flooding his senses with a rush of overwhelming euphoria.

The Hamilton brothers knew they had found something special in the women they had chosen to marry. It was a sense of completion and wholeness that only their partners could provide. That was what Romeo felt in his heart and soul with Daisy Mae.

His tongue slid in between her lips and swept through her mouth, tangling with her tongue. They danced as his mouth covered hers. Her lips were so soft and tasted like she'd applied a peppermint balm to them before heading on the water.

As he entertained that thought, it struck him deeply, causing a visceral reaction as he involuntarily stiffened and pulled back. He realized that he couldn't allow himself to be sidetracked by Daisy Mae if he wanted to ensure her safety in the event of another shooting.

"We best pay attention," he said, attempting to refocus his mind on his surroundings.

She smiled at his discreet adjustment of himself in his shorts. "We be okay." She pointed to his sidearm. "We be okay," she repeated.

Standing on deck, facing away from the island, they gazed toward the water, the peaceful bayou stretching before them. Thankfully, it was an empty waterway—no trouble in sight.

As the boys scrambled to pinpoint the exact location of the treasure and swiftly bring it aboard their waiting boat, a sense of urgency filled the air between Daisy Mae and Romeo. They needed to depart quickly, and their goal was to make a hasty departure before any potential trouble could find them.

When a signal flare launched from the island, he knew it was too late.

Chapter Thirty-One

ROMEO WAS ACUTELY aware that the brothers would not launch the signal flare unless the situation were dire, as they were keen on keeping their location concealed. Acting instinctually, he swiftly dropped his sidearm and tore off his shirt before considering Daisy Mae's safety.

When he turned to her, he saw her one-piece swimsuit, from which she had already removed her top and shorts. "I be coming," she said.

Torn between exposing her to potential danger or leaving her to face it alone, Romeo ultimately decided to bring her along. He believed that by staying together, he would have a better chance of protecting her. Additionally, he considered the possibility that someone might be injured and need assistance rather than facing imminent danger. These thoughts gave him hope as they pressed on.

Daisy Mae grabbed the boat key and then turned to him. "Let's go."

With a warm smile, Romeo gestured for her to dive into the water ahead of him. He couldn't help but admire her grace and elegance as he extended his arm. He needed to keep a close watch on her every movement as they made their way to shore.

Upon reaching the island, Romeo felt grateful for wearing aqua shoes, as the terrain was densely covered with lush vegetation. They briskly followed the partly formed trail created by those who had ventured through the island before them, allowing Romeo and Daisy Mae to navigate the island easily.

Going further than he'd been on the previous excursion with the brothers, Romeo's insides began to knot, and his gut tightened. Something was wrong, and he only hoped to keep Daisy Mae from running headlong into trouble.

As he mulled it over, he became increasingly aware of the magnitude of their problem. His certainty grew when he heard a boat swiftly approaching in the bayou. *Merde.* How could he ensure Daisy Mae's safety with his firearm on the boat? He had been so concerned about what had happened to one of the crew onshore that he hadn't taken the time to put his weapon in a waterproof bag like Alice had done to bring ashore with him.

He longed to have the time to return to the boat and retrieve the weapon, recognizing its crucial importance. Although the danger to Daisy Mae appeared to have dissipated in the bayou, he couldn't shake the feeling that another threat loomed ahead. "*Merde*," he muttered under his breath, feeling the weight of the decision ahead as he stood at a crucial crossroads.

Romeo reached out to Daisy Mae. "Stop."

"*Mais,* why?" Daisy Mae asked as she turned to him, concern for her brothers etched on her face.

"Something be wrong."

"I know. Dat be why we rush."

He shook his head. "No, something be wrong with dis situation."

"We need to find me *frères* before that *bateau* stops at the island."

He found himself filled with increasing uncertainty. Despite his misgivings, he could only cling to hope that his suspicions were unfounded and that a member of the crew had indeed suffered an injury and not a threat to their life.

"Let's go," she insisted and was off before Romeo could stop her.

He hurried behind Daisy Mae to catch up to her jog through the brush to where the flare had been launched. She tripped and fell, and he helped her up.

"You be okay?" He knew the vegetation could be sharp.

Daisy Mae wiped her hands off on her swimsuit and nodded. "Let's go."

However, Romeo noticed her limping a bit as she hurried and saw spots of blood where she had stepped. He wanted to stop and wrap her wound to protect it from the sand but knew she was single-minded and focused on getting to her brothers. They were close, so he could bind it when they checked on her brothers.

As they neared the area, they exited the vegetation to a sandy inlet where Alice met them with her weapon pointed at the brothers while Marie tied Pierre up, JP lying on the ground with blood on his head.

Merde. He could have avoided putting Daisy Mae in this dangerous situation if he had only trusted his gut feeling and followed his instincts. It seemed likely that JP had been struck after he fired the flare to warn them, but rather foolishly, they misinterpreted it as a distress signal of a different kind.

"JP!" Daisy Mae cried and began toward her brother.

"Stop," Alice ordered, turning her gun on Daisy Mae.

"You no shoot me," Daisy Mae said and continued forward.

Alice turned the weapon fully on Romeo. "*Mais,* I would him."

Daisy Mae suddenly stopped, her eyes filled with anguish as she grappled with the impossible choice between saving him and meeting her brother's urgent need. The torment in her eyes was unmistakable as she weighed the options. Finally, he let out a breath he hadn't realized he was holding when she decided to spare his life, fully aware that Alice might not have shown the same mercy.

"Why ya do dis?" Daisy Mae asked.

Romeo was convinced that Daisy Mae's friend held them at gunpoint out of sheer greed. He believed Alice and Marie were solely interested in keeping the treasure for themselves, leading to this extreme and dangerous situation.

"'Cause we deserve it for staying in dis town," Alice said.

Romeo vented his frustration, harshly condemning himself and the other men for not targeting the women as potential suspects first. The exhaustive investigation covered virtually every town resident except Alice, Marie, and Shelly. They could not fathom the possibility of betrayal from Alice—the law—considering her close bond with Daisy Mae. He still couldn't comprehend it from Shelly, who he was sure to be arriving shortly.

"Do something. Da bitches be crazy," Pierre said before Marie backhanded him, and he fell over in the sand.

Romeo found himself in a precarious situation, with Alice holding a weapon. He couldn't afford to underestimate the danger she posed, especially considering the potential risk to Daisy Mae. Despite the stakes, Romeo was relentless in his determination to take action. He deliberated meticulously, considering every possible course of action in search of the best approach to maximize their chances of success. However, now, Alice had the upper hand, so he had to follow orders.

Alice waved the gun toward JP and Pierre. "Over dere, both of ya." Then, to her sister, "Tie dem up."

"Daisy Mae, too?" Marie asked as if in disbelief.

"She be hurt," Romeo said, hoping that would free her from being tied up, leaving someone to untie them when they were left on the island.

Alice's expression briefly shifted to one of concern as she scanned Daisy Mae, her eyes catching the sight of blood on the sand around her. After a moment, Alice reassuredly remarked, "She be fine."

Daisy Mae swayed, and Romeo could see that she was struggling. He was particularly concerned about the sand that had gotten into a cut on her foot, as it posed a serious risk of infection. Romeo was afraid that if they immobilized her and left her alone, as he suspected they might, Daisy Mae's condition could deteriorate rapidly.

He urgently needed to find a way to free them before Shelly arrived. Hope was fading fast as Alice turned her head to talk to Marie. Suddenly, Romeo launched himself at Alice, and in the chaos of the struggle, the gun fired as they tumbled to the sand.

Chapter Thirty-Two

DAISY MAE'S PIERCING scream shattered the peaceful beach sounds, echoing across the inlet as her heart raced. Frozen in shock, she stood motionless, her eyes fixated on Steve and Alice, who were tumbling to the sand in the aftermath of a single gunshot. In that moment of confusion and dread, the question loomed large: which one of them had been shot?

As blood began to stain the sand, she felt herself on the verge of losing control. Even with one of them injured, Steve and Alice continued to struggle in their fight for the gun.

When Marie approached and attempted to separate Steve from Alice, Daisy Mae sprang into action. She leaped onto Marie's back, vehemently trying to prevent her from getting involved in the altercation. As they tumbled backward, Daisy Mae briefly struggled before wriggling from under Marie. Both regained their footing at the exact moment.

Daisy Mae quickly glanced at Steve and Alice to ensure Steve was still distracted, then lunged at Marie.

Caught off guard, Marie stumbled and fell onto the soft sand, leaving Daisy Mae with an opening to strike her with a powerful punch to the jaw.

Merde. Daisy Mae winced as shooting pain jolted up her arm, causing her to shake her hand to alleviate the discomfort. Gradually regaining her composure, she noticed Marie rising to her feet. The two opponents cautiously circled each other, focusing solely on the other, seemingly indifferent to the ongoing altercation nearby.

Daisy Mae urged, "Leave 'em be," feeling torn between wanting to step in herself and trusting Steve to handle the situation. The knowledge that Alice had received training as a sheriff's deputy and was skilled in combat made her uneasy, as she feared they might be evenly matched in a confrontation.

With determination in her voice, Marie squinted her eyes and said, "Sorry, *chère*. No can do." Swiftly, she surged forward, and another shot echoed in the air.

Daisy Mae and Marie froze. Daisy Mae's heart pounded as she waited to see who would emerge unscathed from the intense scuffle.

Steve rolled off Alice while groaning and clutching his side. Blood trickled through his fingers, adding to the tension of the moment.

Daisy Mae darted forward in pursuit of Alice, who'd regained her footing and ran, but Marie slyly extended her foot, causing Daisy Mae to stumble and fall face-first into the warm sand.

Before Daisy Mae could stand, Alice and Marie swiftly dashed toward the shore, heading for Marie's boat. Reacting quickly, Daisy Mae sprang to her feet in hot pursuit of the pair, determined not to allow her so-called friends to leave the four stranded on the island.

However, she heard Steve say, "Leave 'em be. I need ya help to stop da bleeding."

She abruptly stopped and returned to him, tears welling in her eyes. Blood trickled down from his wounded leg and also stained his side, causing a sense of urgency and concern to grip her heart.

"Don't worry, Rocket, da side be a scrape. Da leg needs attention, if you please."

As Daisy Mae frantically worked to apply pressure to the wounds on both Steve's side and leg, she heard the distinct sound of a boat's motor slowly fading away into the distance. The sound made her heart sink as she realized that her so-called friends had fled with their only means of escape.

They discovered themselves stranded on a mysterious and unexplored island nestled within a scarcely traversed waterway deep within the bayou. Daisy Mae was left pondering their chances of being rescued. With no clear plan in mind, she couldn't fathom how they would manage to rescue themselves.

After applying first aid to stop Steve's bleeding, she untied her brothers and went to check on JP, who had regained consciousness. "I feel so foolish. I trusted 'em," she lamented.

"It be okay," JP said. "We did, too."

JP pulled his cell phone, in a waterproof cover, from his pocket. "No bars."

Daisy Mae furrowed her brow and inquired, "Now dat we be here, how are we gonna find a way to get home?"

At that exact moment, the sound of the approaching boat that had been getting closer to the island earlier suddenly ceased. She had assumed it was a rescuer coming to aid Marie and Alice, but now a creeping dread made her wonder if it was the same people returning to complete a sinister task. Fear gripped her as she contemplated the possible threat looming ahead.

Steve lay on his back, surrounded by the eerie silence of the deserted wilderness. He released a heavy sigh that echoed through the stillness. "It must be our rescue party," he muttered with a tinge of hope in his voice despite the dire situation.

Daisy Mae, bewildered, gazed at him in disbelief. "How can ya be so sure, especially since no one even knows we be here?" she said, her concern growing as she approached him again. "Ya must be delirious from blood loss," she added softly, her worry palpable.

"Trust me." He pulled his cell phone from his pocket, nestled in a waterproof cover. That didn't phase Daisy Mae because they had no signal.

"Bat signal," Steve said and then promptly passed out.

Daisy Mae hurried back to Steve's side, panic evident in her voice. "Help me, JP and Pierre. We need to find a place to hide from dis new threat."

JP hesitated, considering the possibility. "What if it be a rescue party?" he asked as he stepped forward to assist in moving the unconscious Steve.

Her voice trembled with fear as she exclaimed, "How dat be possible? No one knows we be here 'cept Marie and Alice. Dey might have dispatched someone to come and eliminate us. 'Member, dat *bateau* was already headed to da island. It must've spotted deir *bateau*. Why did dey not turn around? Why did dey come here? I tell you, we must find a place to hide."

JP and Pierre swiftly gathered Steve, and together, they made their way to a patch of dense brush near the inlet to conceal themselves. After that, Daisy Mae grabbed a piece of vegetation to cover the blood and hide their tracks before seeking cover with the rest of the group.

The island was shrouded in an eerie silence devoid of animal noises or footsteps. Daisy Mae couldn't shake the feeling that someone might be waiting at the boat for her and the others to reach the shore. She was riddled with anxiety over her choice to conceal herself and pondered the uncertain events that lay ahead.

They waited for what felt like forever. Right when Daisy Mae had been about to say that one of them should go to the shore and see what was happening, two women emerged from the trail, rifles raised, surveying the area.

"They're not here," one said as she lowered her weapon.

The other searched the area. "They've been here. Look how they tried to cover the blood."

Just at that moment, Steve let out a pained groan as the woman swiftly advanced in their direction, brandishing their weapons. Daisy Mae felt a sinking feeling of dread as she realized they were in serious trouble and could not defend themselves. The only glimmer of hope she had was that Shelly was not one of them. At least one of her friends hadn't turned their back on her.

"Come out," the taller woman directed. "With your hands where we can see them."

Chapter Thirty-Three

AS ROMEO SLOWLY stirred from unconsciousness, he was surprised to find Daisy Mae lying protectively over him, her soft expression veiling a sense of urgency. As his eyes fluttered open, she gestured for him to remain silent by placing a gentle finger over her lips. His heart raced with concern, wondering what events had transpired in his unconsciousness.

As he scanned his surroundings to regain his bearings, he caught sight of Daisy Mae's brothers concealed in the dense underbrush. The sight immediately triggered a pressing question: who were they hiding from? It seemed improbable that they had managed to elude Alice while transporting his unconscious body.

Alice. Romeo was astounded by the woman's unexpected skills and strength during the wrestling match, leaving him feeling like a complete underdog. It was the first time he had ever found himself in a wrestling match with a gun involved. He dreaded having to concede to the other agents that he had not only been defeated but by a woman who was smaller in stature than he was.

The melodious sound that greeted his ears gently roused him. Kate gestured for them to display their hands.

As he opened his mouth to speak, Daisy Mae swiftly covered it with her hand, her eyes filled with urgency, silently begging him to remain quiet. It suddenly dawned on him that she was unaware they were the rescue party. From the boat, he had managed to send a distress signal to Devon as soon as he realized something was amiss. Doubt lingered in his mind about whether the signal had been successfully transmitted, but he had provided them with crucial information about the island.

His hand reached up, gently removing hers. "Trust me," he whispered to Daisy Mae. Fear gripped her as she shook her head in disbelief. Nevertheless, he was determined to show her that he was right on this one.

"It be me, *chère*," he murmured wearily.

"Oh shit," Kate said, moving toward them.

Rylee did likewise.

Romeo reassured Daisy Mae and her brothers, saying, "Don't worry. Dey be da rescue party. Everything be okay."

Daisy Mae hesitated but eventually rose from atop him in response to his encouraging gesture.

"Show 'em where we be hiding," he requested.

After a nod, she stood, and his two friends appeared.

"You must be Daisy Mae," Kate said warmly. "I'm Kate Hamilton, and this is my sister-in-law, Rylee Hamilton. It appears we're a bit late in helping you out."

Romeo observed Daisy Mae visibly relax as she uttered, "It be all right. Ya, be here now. Steve be badly injured."

Despite his words, "I be fine. Just need a bit of help standing," his voice betrayed the lie, revealing his true struggle.

"Yeah, I can tell you're fine," Rylee laughed. "The blood says it all. Tell us."

Upon realizing that honesty was his only recourse, he uttered, "The injury on me side be merely a graze. However, the pain in me leg be excruciating."

Daisy Mae informed them, "I tried to stop the bleeding."

"You handled that well," Kate reassured her, placing a comforting hand on her shoulder. Moments like these made Kate's intuition and support genuinely invaluable.

Steve furrowed his brow, scanning the group and noticing Grits, Casper, and Devon's absence. Concern etched his features as he asked, "Where be da boys?" It occurred to him that Devon would never have allowed Rylee to come to Louisiana without him and Grits and Casper wouldn't leave him stranded.

Rylee indicated towards the shore. "Devon has detained two hotheads on the boat." Then she gestured at the two figures approaching. "And these two went around the back of the island, just in case."

He felt immense relief knowing that HIS had captured the woman who had shot him and abandoned him, his woman, and her brothers to perish on a remote island. As he regained his strength, he pondered what retribution he would seek against Alice and Marie.

Rylee's eyes shifted back and forth between the twins, JP and Pierre. "You must be JP and Pierre," she said. "Can you tell me which one of you is JP?"

JP stepped forward. "I be him."

Rylee stepped toward him and gently said, "Let me check your head. I understand from the women on the boat that you were hit hard enough to knock you unconscious."

JP extended his hands before him and confidently stated, "I be fine. I no need to be checked out."

Rylee stopped, her expression quizzical as she arched a questioning brow. Romeo was keenly aware of her unspoken thought—the exasperation of dealing with stubborn men. After all, she had encountered plenty of them at HIS.

"Okay, then," Kate said. "Let's get Romeo to his feet and return to the boat. Grits. Casper."

JP and Pierre hurriedly bent down to assist Romeo in standing up after his injury, but Grits firmly waved them away with a reassuring smile. "You've been injured. Let us take care of this," he insisted.

Despite their initial reluctance, the twins eventually conceded and reluctantly stepped away, exchanging concerned glances as they yielded to Grit's determined demeanor.

"Boy, when you do things, you do them big," Casper said.

Romeo grunted his response.

The men gently eased him into a sitting position, causing Romeo's side to bleed, but he brushed off the concern. Instead, his mind was preoccupied with the daunting task of standing on his injured leg. Summoning his courage, he attempted. The men effortlessly hoisted his dead weight with impressive strength, lifting him until he could finally stand.

Merde. It was excruciatingly painful, but deep down, Romeo was confident it wasn't too serious. Despite lacking medical expertise, he could sense it in his very being. As he cautiously reached the back of his leg, the sensation of blood confirmed his fears. It was a through-and-through shot, but he found solace in that it hadn't lodged itself in the bone, considering it a small victory amid adversity.

"Let's get you home," Kate said tenderly.

Romeo's heart fluttered with hope, but he couldn't shake the fear of returning to Baltimore. His real home might be here with Daisy Mae. He longed to convince her to take a leap of faith with him, to embark on a new journey and build a life together. It was a daunting request, but he was ready to go to great lengths for her.

The seemingly endless journey back to the boat felt arduous. Grits and Casper carefully supported him, preventing unintentional pressure on his injured leg. Maneuvering through the sparsely cleared trail was precarious. Suddenly, a snake dropped before them, bouncing off Romeo's legs. He almost pissed himself, realizing the potential venomous threat posed by the snakes in the vicinity.

"Watch it," he hissed to the men holding him.

"What, scared of a little snake?" Grits joked.

If Romeo had been capable of doing so, he would have hit Grits in response to that remark. Romeo felt powerless, sandwiched between two men, without defending himself. *Merde.* He urgently needed to get to the boat.

Kate and Rylee stood before him, firing off a barrage of questions about the recent events at Daisy Mae. Initially hesitant, Daisy Mae finally opened up and candidly answered all their questions, providing them with the missing information.

Several feet behind the women, Casper asked, "What will you do about her?"

"I know not what ya be talking 'bout," he responded, lying his ass off. *Merde*. He planned to take her home with him or remain here. Whatever it took.

Upon arrival, Romeo was stunned to find Mario's boat patiently waiting for them, with Mario seated confidently in the captain's chair.

At the sight of Mario, Daisy Mae asked angrily, "What he be here for?"

"He was the only one available, and he offered to help," Devon remarked as he turned toward them. Marie and Alice sat on the boat's bench with their hands cuffed.

"*Chère*, dere be no hard feelings between us. I hear what happened, and I wanted to help, me," Mario said. He launched a small inflatable boat with determined strides and began paddling to shore, his grip firm on the oar.

Romeo expressed immense gratitude upon seeing the inflatable boat launched, as the thought of how he would have managed to swim to the boat was daunting. Upon reaching the shore, Daisy Mae watched Grits and Casper assist Romeo as he boarded the small boat. Inside the craft, with limited space that accommodated only him, Daisy Mae, Mario, and the ladies' weapons, they embarked on their journey toward Mario's boat. The others took to the water to swim to the boat.

Daisy Mae maintained a vigilant gaze on him, her disapproving expression directed at Mario. "*Merci*," she eventually expressed to her former adversary.

"It no ting," Mario responded, his skin glistening with sweat as he labored to row the boat.

Once they reached Mario's boat, Devon offered Romeo a hand as he carefully helped him into the larger vessel. Every movement aggravated the pain in Romeo's leg, and the blood had already seeped through his shorts and stained his leg. However, thankfully, the bleeding had stopped for the time being.

Devon surveyed Romeo's injuries and sighed. "In addition to locating the jailhouse, we must find a hospital." Knowing that Devon had more medical training than the other team members, Romeo silently hoped that his expression wouldn't reveal the severity of his injuries.

Mario and Daisy Mae worked harmoniously to secure the inflatable to the boat, double-checking the knots to ensure its security. Once everything was in place and everyone was aboard, they carefully launched and embarked on their journey back to civilization.

Devon's voice was tinged with frustration as he spoke, "So, you were supposed to wait for us. You're lucky we found you."

Romeo was deeply troubled by the prospect that this incident could spiral into Devon forcibly implanting everyone with tracking devices, eliminating their privacy and freedom. Despite the group's resistance, Devon was adamant about implementing this invasive surveillance, citing the challenges of locating them. While some suggested wearing tracking devices only during operations, Devon argued that they would need to be always worn, emphasizing how often individuals found themselves in dangerous situations when left to their own devices, an increasingly evident trend lately.

Romeo was indifferent at the time. All he wanted was to find a doctor and rest, but he resisted doing so while he was with Daisy Mae. Perhaps he felt the need to display a sense of toughness around her, but he wouldn't allow her to witness any more of his pain than she already had.

"Romeo," Kate said with narrowed, watchful eyes, "you don't look so good."

"I be fine, *chère*," he said before he passed out on the deck.

Chapter Thirty-Four

DAISY MAE SAT next to Steve's hospital bed with her eyes fixed on him and worry etched into her expression. He had just undergone minor surgery to extract debris and bullet fragments from a wound on his leg, with the incision meticulously sealed. Although not life-threatening, the injury was substantial enough, causing him to limp for an extended period as it had grazed the bone and muscle.

She found herself in a quandary. This morning, she spoke with the insurance agent, only to learn that they were unwilling to offer her the total value of her boat. Purchasing a new one would deplete most of her savings, and with her business in Bayou Junction, it would be a considerable amount of time before she could recover from the financial setback.

However, her life, in general, was at stake, and Steve had not requested that she accompany him to Baltimore. His intentions initially seemed different, as if he wanted more from her, but it became evident that all he desired was a fleeting encounter.

Kate informed her they had already arranged a plane to take them home when he was discharged from the hospital later today. However, Daisy Mae hadn't been invited to join the trip. Then again, why would she be? She wasn't part of the group.

She jolted out of her thoughts when Steve groaned, "*Merde.*"

She stood up from her seat, at a loss for words. "I go get da nurse. dey wanted to know when ya woke," she said as she rushed out of the room. She couldn't help but wonder why she was feeling so timid.

As she exited, she heard him say, "Daisy Mae," but she didn't stop to see what he said. He probably had the same regrets as she did. Their affair had been a dream since they were younger. Now, as adults, it didn't work. They lived two separate lives in two separate parts of the country.

When she found the nurse, she went to the waiting room to update Steve's colleagues about his awakening. Kate had been engrossed in a phone call while Devon and Rylee were huddled together, deep in conversation. Grits and Casper had taken Marie and Alice to the sheriff's department and were tying up loose ends elsewhere.

The three of them immediately stopped what they were doing and eagerly rose to see Steve. Sensing their eagerness, she quickly intervened, reminding them that the nurse and doctor should first see Steve.

"They'll keep him overnight for observation," Devon said in general conversation. "Assuming the sheriff clears him to leave, I've rescheduled us for wheels up at 1600 hours tomorrow."

Knowing it still didn't include her, Daisy Mae sat and ignored the timeline with Steve as best she could. She realized the sheriff hadn't made it there yet. She expected him to ask questions even if she couldn't answer them.

She must've looked worried because Kate said, "Don't worry. Grits and Casper are keeping him away until after Romeo awoke."

Daisy Mae felt a sharp pang whenever she heard Steve called "Romeo." It was different when the men called him that—it felt casual, almost harmless. But when the women used it, there was something intimate, nearly piercing, about the way it sounded, cutting through her defenses and leaving her feeling exposed. She knew it was ridiculous but couldn't help how she felt about it.

"And," Rylee said, "here they are."

Upon glancing toward the door, Daisy Mae's eyes fell upon Grits and Casper as they entered the waiting room, with the sheriff close behind. Their faces were lit up with childlike glee as they stepped inside. What followed next took her entirely by surprise. Each of them took a seat, flanking her on either side, effectively cocooning her between them like a pair of devoted guardians.

"Now boys," Sheriff Boudreaux said, "ya know I needs to chat with dis here young lady."

Grits shrugged. "Go ahead."

After a moment, the sheriff sighed and pulled over a chair before her. "*Chère*, how you be?"

She felt nothing but numbness. Her friends, who she trusted completely, had betrayed her. The love of her life, the one person she thought would always be there, was about to leave her. She tried to speak, opening her mouth as if to utter a word, but no sound emerged. What could she possibly say in such a moment of profound hurt?

At that moment, a whirlwind named Shelley breezed into the waiting room.

"Daisy Mae," she said as she hurried forward.

Daisy Mae shot out of her chair like a burst of energy, her feet barely touching the ground as she sped around Sheriff Boudreaux. In an instant, she was enveloped in Shelley's warm embrace, her heart pounding wildly, and only then did the tears stream down her face.

"*Chère*. It's gonna be okay," her friend said softly.

When would it be okay? The pang of regret echoed in her heart as she replayed the time Steve had been home in her mind. She finally had her chance with him, the one she'd dreamt about for so long, and somehow, she'd blown it. The weight of missed opportunities settled on her as she realized he was leaving tomorrow, leaving her behind with a tapestry of what-ifs.

"Now, Shelley—" Sheriff Boudreaux said before Kate cut him off.

"When Romeo wakes, Devon will accompany you back."

Daisy Mae ignored the sheriff's and Kate's heated argument, focusing instead on Shelley's strong embrace and the warmth and comfort absentmindedly provided. Her friend was an unyielding anchor, holding her together amidst the chaos. When her torrent of tears eventually subsided, she reluctantly stepped back. "I needs to get outta here," she murmured, her voice barely above a whisper.

"We can handle that," Casper said from behind her, his sudden voice causing her to jump. At an unknown moment, he had moved closer, enveloping her in his protective presence again. He shielded her from the intimidating sheriff and all potential threats, except the aching void left by Steve's lost love.

With a final glance at the hospital, she nodded and stepped out into the cool evening. The sheriff's stern expression and Rylee's concerned eyes faded into the background. With every step away from the building, the weight of unfamiliar faces and sterile corridors grew lighter. She had no place here among Steve's professional world and supportive friends. Her heart ached, but the freedom of the water called her forward.

When Casper folded himself into the backseat of Shelley's car, his movements were hesitant but purposeful. She felt a lump in her throat, unsure how to break the thickening silence around them. It was a heavy moment, a decisive step towards breaking free from Steve's suffocating world, far away from the ever-watchful eyes of his colleagues.

"Ash. Casper, I mean, I need to be alone now," she stammered, her voice trembling with a mixture of resolve and apprehension.

"That's fine," came his calm reply, yet he made no move to leave the vehicle.

"Den, why ya no be getting out?" she demanded, her confusion growing as she observed the unwavering resolve in his eyes.

"Because you're Romeo's girl, and we look after our own," he stated firmly, with an unshakable conviction that made her chest tighten.

Torn between gratitude and frustration, she turned to face the front, unable to hold back the torrent of emotions any longer. "Drive, Shelley," she murmured, her voice barely holding steady as tears began to blur her vision. Casper's words, though well-intentioned, felt like a cage around her heart. She knew she wasn't Romeo's girl, only a fleeting part of Steve's chaotic world.

She felt the weight of her past as she stood on the brink of a new beginning. The memories of Bayou Junction, a town steeped in her history with Steve, haunted her every step. Her heart, heavy with the sorrows of what once was, ached to break free from the chains of nostalgia. With a deep breath, she resolved to leave everything behind and venture into a place untouched by his memory, where she could rebuild the fragments of her existence and embrace potential anew.

Chapter Thirty-Five

STRUGGLING WITH FRUSTRATION and pain, Romeo lay in the sterile, white hospital bed, his body twisted with discomfort and weariness. The fluorescent lights hummed softly above him, casting an artificial glare over the sheriff's pale features. The sheriff, a grizzled man with a thick mustache and a notepad in hand, fired off a barrage of inane questions that grated on Romeo's nerves. Devon, his loyal friend and one of his bosses, stood at the foot of the bed. Devon's calm demeanor starkly contrasted with the chaos. He stepped in to redirect the sheriff's questions occasionally, his composed voice soothing the tension in the room. Romeo's interview experience shined through as he deftly navigated the conversation, ensuring he only revealed what was absolutely necessary.

Where the hell was Daisy Mae? He'd expected her by his side the entire time he was hospitalized, which was thankfully only overnight. Her absence was palpable, casting a shadow over the room.

He was brimming with anticipation of tracking down Daisy Mae and imploring her to join him in starting a new chapter of their lives together in Baltimore, leaving behind the comforts and memories of his quaint hometown. However, a bittersweet pang tugged at his heart at the thought of parting from his beloved parents. But where were his parents?

An unsettling concern gnawed at him—why hadn't they come to visit him yet? As if his unspoken worries had materialized into words, Devon said reassuringly, "We just sent Grits after your parents. We didn't want them to have to endure the agonizing wait in the hospital's sterile, impersonal waiting room to see you."

The gesture appeared thoughtful, yet perhaps over-the-top. His parents, undoubtedly, would prefer to stay by his side at the hospital, sharing those crucial moments with him. Suddenly, a realization struck him. Had his parents been there, they would have spent those precious minutes beside his hospital bed rather than Daisy Mae. Overwhelmed, his throat tightened almost to the point of choking as he managed to utter, "*Merci, chèr*."

Once the sheriff had reached his limit, his patience threadbare, he turned to Devon with a steely gaze and demanded, "Now, where did *Deyzee Mè* get off to?"

Romeo's instincts flared as he snapped to attention. Daisy Mae had left the hospital? The implications spun in his mind, creating a vortex of worry. He flung off the covers in a swift, determined motion, ready to leave the sterile confines of the hospital bed and pursue the woman he cared for. Ever the vigilant agent, Devon intercepted him. "She just went to see her brothers at Duke's," he explained calmly. "To check on them and let them know she was okay." He paused and met Romeo's anxious gaze. "Casper is with her."

Relief washed over Romeo. Knowing Casper was by her side gave him a sense of peace. He was reassured that she would return to him soon, before he departed, giving him the precious chance to persuade her to restart their journey together.

Before the sheriff departed, a tense silence hung in the air. Romeo's curiosity and concern were evident as he inquired, "Da map? Did it be authentic?"

Sheriff Boudreaux, with a nonchalant demeanor, shrugged in response. "Antionne say so. He plans ta search once he has da permits. So, we be seeing," he said, his voice conveying skepticism and cautious optimism. The room seemed to echo with the weight of their uncertainties as the sheriff stepped out into the hallway.

Once alone with Devon, he looked at him concernedly and asked, "I need to see her."

Devon, his expression grave, shook his head gently. "You need to see your parents." A myriad of emotions flickered across his face; he did need to see his parents. Images of their worried faces and his father's past heart attack flooded his mind. They would be anxious beyond measure unless they could see that he was healing. He couldn't bear the thought of causing them undue stress. Resolute, he took a deep breath and nodded. He'd reunite with Daisy Mae afterward. "Send them in when they be here," he instructed, his voice steady but laden with unspoken concerns.

Straightening the covers meticulously, he waited anxiously for his parents to enter the brightly lit room. The relief he felt that Casper had left with Daisy Mae was palpable. His mind raced with thoughts—she might have gone to purchase her boat. What drove her away so abruptly? Could it truly have been to check on her brothers? She could have easily made a phone call. But JP had sustained a blow to the head; maybe that was why she needed to see him in person. Then again, modern technology offered video chats. Frustration gnawed at him; he yearned for her presence beside him in this trying moment.

His mother rushed into the room, her eyes wide with worry. His father followed her slowly, moved with hesitant steps, a deep furrow of concern etched into his brow. "Steve," his mother said, her voice trembling slightly as she stepped beside his bed, casting a shadow over his pale form lying beneath the thin hospital sheets.

"*Bonjour, Mamau* and Papa," he said, his voice laced with unwavering confidence to alleviate the anxious expressions tugging at his parents' faces.

His mother, her fingers shaking slightly, adjusted the covers on his bed with tender care. Meanwhile, his father moved to the opposite side, his face a mix of worry and relief. "How ya be?" his father inquired, his voice resonating with concern.

Steve managed a nod, offering a brief smile. "*Bien*," he responded, though the word was tinged with exhaustion. The doctor had cautioned him about the fragility of his stitches—they could quickly reopen, both on his side and his leg. He knew he'd have to rely on a cane for the foreseeable future, a constant reminder of his need to keep weight off his injured limb.

"I be sorry," his father said with a weary voice, his eyes burdened with regret. "I got ya dragged into dis mess."

"What on earth ya be talking about?" his mother asked, a puzzled look on her face.

"Papa asked me to keep an eye on Daisy Mae," Romeo explained, his expression growing serious. "And he be right. She needed me and my organization to watch her six."

With a puzzled expression, her mother tilted her head slightly and inquired, "Watch her six?"

Armor-clad in his professional demeanor, Romeo immersed himself deeply into his work mindset, temporarily shelving any thoughts of a vacation with his family. "I'm sorry, *Mamau*. It means watch her back."

Comprehension dawned slowly as she nodded, attempting to appear as though she had grasped the meaning from the start. "Oh," she echoed, her voice a blend of understanding and curiosity. Her eyes darted around, scanning the room with motherly concern. "Where she be? I expected her to be waiting. We needed to see if she be all right."

"She be checking on her *frères*," he said, hoping that was true. She'd seemed distant the last time they were together, as if he'd left her behind while he ventured ahead. Then, a realization jolted through him; she might think he had no intention of bringing her along since he hadn't even hinted at it.

His initial urge was to leap from the bed, driven by an urgent need to see her until he felt his parents in the room. "I need to get out of here," he muttered, a sense of determination rising.

"You needs to rest," his mother said tenderly, her voice laced with worry, while his father added with firm resolve, "I'll get da doctor."

Before they could exchange another word, Casper appeared in the doorway, a grim expression casting a shadow over his features. His clothes were slightly disheveled, a testament to his hurried chase. "She gave me the slip," he announced, frustration evident in his tone.

"How?" Romeo's voice dripped with disbelief, resonating in the small, bright room. This had to be the first time anyone had given Casper the slip. Known as their best tracker, this situation was unprecedented.

"She and Shelley slipped out the back while going to the restroom," came the reluctant reply, the frustration palpable in the air.

Merde. A string of curses ran through Romeo's mind. But he knew he'd catch up with her later at her home. That was inevitable. Devon might have to adjust their wheels-up time, but he wouldn't let her get away. Not without a fight.

Chapter Thirty-Six

AFTER A LONG, somber week lingering on Daisy Mae's doorstep, under the watchful eyes of the neighborhood's blossoming gardens and chirping birds, Romeo came to a heart-wrenching realization. It was a realization that carried the weight of a thousand unspoken words and that it was time to return to work. The scent of fresh blooms couldn't mask the bitter truth: She wouldn't go home as long as he was there, his presence a silent barrier to her return. His heart sank with the weight of a lost love and the vanished dream of a shared life.

Back at headquarters, in the harsh glow of lights and the buzz of non-stop chatter, his team was gearing up for their next high-stakes assignment. He hadn't fully recovered, but they needed everyone on the op, so he assisted Devon.

The absence of Casper—engulfed in a family emergency—was a quiet, solemn note in the team's otherwise focused preparations. They departed on their op, disappearing for three exhaustive weeks, each day stretching into an agonizing eternity for Romeo. A heart-wrenching month slipped by, marked by the relentless ache of missing Daisy Mae and the ghost of unfulfilled possibilities, the slow passage of time only serving to deepen his emotional turmoil.

When the team returned from their op, he felt an overwhelming need for a change of scenery and requested a well-deserved vacation to visit his parents. He harbored a secret hope and excitement about reuniting with Daisy Mae. With a heart full of longing and vivid memories, he planned to see if the spark between them was still alive, believing deep down that her feelings for him remained unchanged.

When he drove into the quiet, sleepy town after the exhaustingly long journey, fatigue bore down heavily on him, but he couldn't give in to rest; he had to see Daisy Mae. His eyes widened with disbelief as his truck pulled up in front of her home. A conspicuous, glaringly "For Sale" sign stood like an omen in the tidy front yard, disrupting the familiar serenity. With a sense of urgent desperation, he jerked open his truck door. Ignoring the creak of exhaustion from his body and vehicle, he dashed to her front door and began pounding urgently. "Daisy Mae," he yelled, his voice tinged with worry and confusion.

When no one answered, a heavy rock of dread formed in his stomach as if tethered to the weight of his growing anxiety. His heart pounded as he shuffled to the windows, peering through the glass with desperate hope. The house was lonely, echoing the emptiness that gnawed at him. He was too late to make amends. His whole world collapsed as realization dawned: she had moved on without him, leaving him adrift in a sea of regret. What was he to do now, with the emptiness threatening to consume him? He needed her like the air he breathed, but she'd fled, leaving nothing but memories and a hollow, aching void.

Under the shimmering glow of the streetlights, he painstakingly made his way to Shelley's home. The late hour cast long shadows, but urgency drove him. Shelley held the answers to Daisy Mae's whereabouts, and he was desperate for any clue. His heart drummed in his chest, each beat a plea for her return.

He envisioned Daisy Mae's laughter echoing over the bayou. Life without her felt like navigating through a never-ending storm, leaving him fractured and incomplete. The world around him was a blur. Only the thought of having her back could bring color to his existence once more.

When Shelley swung open the door, an unexpected fury ignited from her. She propelled herself at him, not with the warmth of an embrace but with the fiery intensity of a confrontation. Her fists rained upon his chest, punctuated by the sharp, accusing words, "She left because of ya." Her declaration tore through the air with each blow, laden with pain and betrayal. Tears cascaded down her face, a torrent of sorrow that diluted her force as she uttered, almost in a whisper, "I don't know where she be."

Romeo stood patiently, allowing her to vent her fury. As her clenched fists pounded against him, he remained calm, absorbing each blow with silent resilience. Once her energy waned and her strikes weakened, he gently enveloped her in a firm embrace, drawing her close. She clung to him desperately as if he were the last anchor in a storm-tossed sea. Leaning down, he whispered into her ear with unwavering determination, "I be going to find her. Even if it be the last thing I do, I will find her."

After her tears subsided, she invited him to come inside. His heart yearned to accept, but the night had grown late, and he still had to visit his parents. A heavy urgency to find Daisy Mae weighed upon his chest like an anchor. The lateness of the hour rendered any effort futile, so he assured Shelley that he would return in the morning for a more thorough conversation. This would allow Shelley to recover from her emotional upheaval and give him a chance to glean information from his parents about Daisy Mae's sudden departure.

Only his parents were also clueless. His mother, a nurturing figure to Daisy Mae akin to an adoptive mother, shed tears over her departure. Romeo pondered whether Daisy Mae understood the pain she inflicted, more significant than his own, as she vanished without a trace, leaving everyone in the dark about her whereabouts.

Her brothers were his final lifeline in uncovering her whereabouts. After bidding his parents goodnight, he set out towards Duke's, hoping to find JP and Pierre. Upon arriving, a wave of nostalgia washed over him, reminiscent of his previous time there.

JP came at him, fury emanating from every pore. "She left because of ya," he growled, his voice seething with rage.

It was a scene from his past playing out again, like a vicious nightmare replay. The déjà vu hit him with the same intensity as JP's punch to his jaw.

Romeo wouldn't fight back; he felt the punishment was justified this time.

Realizing Romeo wouldn't reciprocate, JP didn't swing again, although Romeo could see in his eyes Daisy

Mae's brother wanted to do so. "I want to find her. Do ya know where she be?" This was his last hope.

JP slumped deeply as an immense burden had just been thrust upon his shoulders. His voice trembled, barely audible, as he whispered, "*Non.*"

Pierre, ever the peacemaker with a demeanor as calm as the early morning sea, deftly slid two frosty, amber-colored beers down the length of the polished mahogany bar toward Romeo and JP. JP, his face contorting into a look of disdain, turned his nose up at the offered beverage and strolled away with an air of contempt, putting as much distance as he could from Romeo.

Meanwhile, Romeo, his eyes glinting with curiosity and a need for camaraderie, accepted the beer with a hopeful smile and sat on the tall barstool. However, Pierre, despite being the seemingly ever-present mediator, chose this moment to turn his back and walk away, leaving Romeo alone amidst the chatter and clinking glasses of the dimly lit bar.

Romeo drowned his sorrows in yet another draft beer, the bitter taste mirroring his heartache. She'd left without a word to anyone, disappearing like a wisp of smoke. He'd never find her now, his dreams of a happily-ever-after slipping away, much like the Hamilton brothers had found.

As the evening progressed, the bar began to empty, with just a few scattered patrons nursing their grief. Someone silently took a seat beside him at the empty bar. Before he could gather the energy to ask the figure to move, Casper's familiar voice broke the silence, saying, "Do you want to know?"

Chapter Thirty-Seven

DAISY MAE DETESTED the impersonal nature of scheduling charters online. She preferred the comfort of face-to-face interactions, where she could see and judge the character of the person she was booking. Something was reassuring about the old-school method, a sense of security that had safeguarded her for years, giving her the intuition to know when to decline a request.

Now, she had a request from one passenger who paid a substantial premium for her time and went by the name of John Smith. Though it was a common enough name, she doubted its authenticity, a suspicion that gnawed at her and added a layer of unease to the charter.

The past few months spent in the windswept, languidly charming town of Lake Charles, Louisiana, had been a tumultuous balm for her bruised heart. Well, if she were being honest, it hadn't been healing at all—in fact, it had only deepened her sorrow and made the ache more acute. Her thoughts drifted often, wondering if Steve, with his rugged charm and piercing hazel eyes, had ever considered coming back for her. Doubt crept in like an uninvited guest, and this gnawing uncertainty amplified her heartache, a cruel reminder that, for him, their bond had never held the same weight it did for her.

As the two men approached her boat, she couldn't help but notice the sizable cooler they were carrying. Immediately, her senses heightened, and she was poised, ready to react. Two men? The unsettling thought of a possible deception regarding the charter arrangement gnawed at her.

With an air of formality, the men requested permission to board and unload their cargo, gesturing towards the imposing white cooler.

Cargo? Her anxiety surged. Contemplating aborting the cruise, her attention was suddenly drawn to a familiar figure in a black baseball cap trailing behind the men. That recognizable cap could only belong to one person— Steve had tracked her down.

Her heart pounded like a drum reverberating in an empty hall, its rhythm quickening with each passing moment. An intense urge overwhelmed her, compelling her to sprint forward and throw herself into his arms. But then, a question shattered the tender fantasy. What was he doing here? Was he here to profess his undying love for her, to mend the broken pieces of her heart? Or had he been sent on a cold, calculated mission by her family to bring her back into their controlling grasp?

Doubt snaked through her veins, seeping into her very being and reviving the dormant ache of abandonment and uncertainty.

The two men grunted as they dropped the chest onto her vessel. Without uttering a word, they disembarked from her boat, their boots clanging against the metal gangplank. As they trudged away, they each patted Steve firmly on the shoulders, their hands lingering briefly, and offered a gruff, "Good luck."

Steve stood on the edge of the pier and removed his black cap. "*Bonjour*, Daisy Mae," he called out, his voice carrying over the rhythmic lapping of the waves against her boat's hull.

"Steve," was all she could mutter, her voice barely above a whisper. Was he her John Smith for this charter, which she would conduct alone for two hours? The realization hit her like a tidal wave. She needed to cancel to end this before anything more was said or emotions became entangled. Yet, the words seemed to lodge in her throat, refusing to be spoken.

"May I board?" he asked.

Without hesitation, she nodded. Her heart raced, and she wanted to kick herself for the swift, almost automatic agreement. Her breath caught in her throat as she watched him move.

Steve, a tall figure casting a long shadow in the morning sun, replaced the cap on his short-cropped hair and stepped onto the vessel. The boat swayed ever so slightly with his step, the wood groaning softly under his weight. The air felt cool against their skin, a sharp contrast to the warm hues of the dawn enveloping them.

"I have a charter scheduled. Sorry for the deception, but I feared ya might not speak with me since ya ran away," he said, his voice carrying a mix of regret and concern as he approached her, his footsteps echoing softly.

Ire climbed up her body to rest on her shoulders like a weight pressing down, tightening her muscles. *Run away?* She did not run away. Okay, maybe she did, but she would not admit it, not even to herself. "I no run away, Steve. It be time to find a new *bateau* and place to dock it," she stated, her voice firm yet betraying a hint of defensiveness, her eyes avoiding his.

"Why ya no do dat in Bayou Junction?" he asked, advancing methodically toward her.

She took a cautious step back, a wave of uncertainty mingling with the recollection of the fabricated story she'd devised for such an occasion. "Dere not be enough business dere," she replied, her voice wavering slightly.

He closed the distance, compelling her to retreat further until her back pressed against the rough wood of the captain's quarters door.

"And, ya had to do it without telling anyone where ya go?" he pressed, another step eliminating the space between them.

She'd loathed not informing her family of her new home, but she had resolved to disclose her whereabouts after a few more months. The fear of someone tracing her steps and persuading her to return to a place filled with sorrow weighed heavily on her mind.

"What do ya want, Steve?" she demanded curtly, her voice tinged with frustration.

"Well, Rocket, da answer be simple. I want ya," he declared, enclosing her with his arms, one on each side of the wooden wall behind her head. "I've always wanted ya."

Her heart soared like an eagle at his admission, an intoxicating mixture of joy and disbelief causing her to still. She longed to leap into his arms, to feel his reassuring embrace, but a whisper of caution anchored her feet to the ground. "Why now?" she asked, her voice barely more than a breath.

"Because I only just found ya," he replied with a hint of sorrow. "Ya be gone before."

If she hadn't rushed away, would he have sought her out? Would he have whisked her away to Maryland or remained steadfast in Bayou Junction? So many questions swirled like a storm in her mind. Now was the time to demand answers.

"So, ya found me. Now what?" she queried, her eyes searching his intently.

"Well, we go on dis here cruise and decide if ya come home wit me or if I move here wit ya. It be dat simple. We no return until it be decided one way or da other," he stated firmly.

With a burst of emotion, she launched herself at him, almost knocking him to the ground. Her heart swelled with a profound love for this man, a love that seemed to defy ordinary bounds.

"We no need to go on da charter," she murmured, her voice soft yet resolute. "I go with ya, wherever ya be."

He wrapped her in a warm embrace, his lips hovering just above hers. "I love ya, Daisy Mae Robicheaux," he whispered fervently.

"I love ya, Steve Smith. My Romeo," she replied, her voice filled with tender affection.

His lips brushed hers in a searing kiss that ignited an undeniable spark and claimed her heart as his own. With a breathless fervor, she kissed him back, her senses belonging solely to him. Their passionate embrace only broke when a roar of cheers erupted from the dock, reverberating around them.

Embarrassed, she ducked her head, feeling the heat rise in her cheeks, and peeked shyly up at the pier. There stood several men, the only familiar face being Grits. "What be going on?" she asked, her eyes searching his.

Steve's grin radiated confidence. "Backup. Just in case ya no agree."

A mix of confusion and curiosity swirled within her. "What were dey gonna do? Drag me away?"

Steve chuckled, a glint of determination in his eyes. "Well, they do have my six. They'd do whatever was necessary to ensure we be together." He put his arm around her waist and turned her to the men. "Welcome to the family," he told her.

About The Author

SHEILA KELL writes about romantic men who leave women's hearts pounding with a happily ever after built on memorable, adrenaline-pumping stories. She is a four-time winner of the Readers' Favorite Book Award for romantic and contemporary suspense.

As a Southern girl who has left behind her days with the United States Air Force and as a University Vice President, she can usually be found in South Mississippi, where she lives with her cats and all the strays that magically find her front door. When she isn't writing, you can find Sheila with her nose in a good book, dealing with the woodland critters who enjoy her back porch, or wishing she had a genie to do her bidding.

Ways to connect

https://www.sheilakellbooks.com

https://www.facebook.com/sheilakellbooks

https://www.goodreads.com/sheilakellbooks

https://www.bookbub.com/authors/sheila-kell

Sheila loves to hear directly from readers. Feel free to email her at sheila@sheilakell.com.

Don't miss out on new releases, exclusive excerpts, and giveaways!
Join her newsletter:
https://www.SheilaKell.com/subscribe
Join her Facebook Reader Group:
https://www.facebook.com/groups/sheilakellbooks

www.ingramcontent.com/pod-product-compliance
Lightning Source LLC
Chambersburg PA
CBHW011136190726
48289CB00012B/3064